HIS TO CLAIM

SIERRA CARTWRIGHT

HIS TO CLAIM

First E-book Publication: January 2019

Editor: Nicki Richards, What's Your Story Editorial Services

Line Editing by Jennifer Barker

Proofing by Bev Albin and Cassie Hess-Dean

Layout Design by Once Upon An Alpha, Shannon Hunt

Cover Design by Once Upon An Alpha, Shannon Hunt

Photographer: Annie Ray at Passion Pages

Cover Model: Dillion Lalor

Photo provided by Annie Ray/Passion Pages

Promotion by Once Upon An Alpha, Shannon Hunt

It is a standalone with my guarantee of satisfying happily ever after.

Created with Vellum

Especially for the sprint group that motivates and encourages, inspires and kicks ass. Thank you, Shayla, Jenna, Stacey, Angel, Elle, and Shayla F. You help me get more done, and I appreciate the brainstorming and the way you're so generous with sharing ideas. Your friendship is a gift I cherish.

BAB, I have no idea what I would do without you.

And to you. I appreciate your taking the time to drop me a line to say hello and share your stories with me.

CHAPTER 1

There were a hell of a lot better ways Mason could be spending his Friday night. Watching a documentary on television, for example. Doing woodwork in his shop. Putting together ideas for his upcoming pitch to a home and garden network for a renovation show.

Instead, not looking forward to the evening, Mason pushed through the door that led from the stairs to the reception area of the Quarter, New Orleans' most exclusive BDSM club.

Because of the large number of guests arriving for tonight's charity slave auction, Aviana, the owner, was helping the receptionist check people in. When she spotted him, she smiled. A moment later, she excused herself and rounded the podium to greet him. "Mason!"

"Milady." He raised her hand to his lips. "Radiant, as always."

Tonight, the tall, willowy woman looked fierce, every bit the Mistress she was. Her boots snuggled her thighs, and the heels sent her soaring past six feet tall. Her two-piece outfit was sensational. The skirt and cropped jacket-type top were brown leather armor and adorned with hundreds of metal pyramid spikes. Her long hair was piled on top of her head, and silver pins were stabbed into it, making sure none of the strands dared attempt an escape.

"You look dashing," she said, smoothing one of his lapels.

"It's rented."

"Your secret is safe with me."

It wasn't a secret. Mason spent his days in blue jeans, well-worn boots, and T-shirts as he visited his job sites. When he had the chance, he swung the hammer himself.

"I didn't expect to see you."

"You…" He cleared his throat. *Coerced.* "Convinced me."

She smiled with obvious triumph.

To be fair, he owed her the show of support. They both served on the board of a charity his father had started, rehabilitating homes for the city's elderly population. And once a year, Aviana hosted a fundraiser that helped make their work possible. He'd skipped last year's event, and she'd made a point of mentioning that fact at each of their monthly meetings ever since.

Still, this was the last place he wanted to be. He preferred to visit the Quarter on those rare occasions when he desired the connection with a submissive.

"Program?" Aviana offered, taking one of the folded pieces of paper from the top of the podium.

He shook his head. "That won't be necessary. Thanks." Mason had no intention of bidding on any of the women participating in the slave auction.

"Who knows? Perhaps you might be tempted."

To spend an entire weekend with a woman he'd purchased? Not likely. It had been more than two years since he'd invited anyone to share his bed. He checked his watch. "What time can I escape?"

"The festivities should end around midnight."

"Drinks being served?"

"The bar is closed until the auction ends."

He generally appreciated her rules. Right now? Not so much. The next few hours would be much easier with a nice bourbon.

A crowd entered the foyer, filling the space with laughter.

"We'll catch up later?" she suggested. "Perhaps lunch within the next couple of weeks?"

"As long as it's friendly, with no written agenda."

"Of course."

He eyed her suspiciously, unsure whether she was telling the truth.

Aviana turned away, then stopped to look back over her shoulder. "I'm glad you came."

He gave her a half smile. It was the best he could manage. Until he picked up the tux a few hours ago, he hadn't been sure he'd actually attend.

Mason pushed through the frosted-glass door leading to the dungeon that was filled with loud, thumping music, no doubt meant to excite the crowd.

The first thing he noticed was Aviana's throne, placed on a raised dais off to one side where she could lord over the event.

All the usual play equipment had been removed from the area. The Saint Andrew's crosses were lined up against the walls, with spanking benches placed in front of them.

A stage had been erected at the far end of the room. Never one to do things by half measures, Aviana had hired lighting and camera crews and had positioned two large screens at angles so that all attendees would have a good view.

Comfortable padded chairs had been arranged in precise rows for the bidders and gawkers who'd paid Aviana's exorbitant admission fee. He knew exactly how much it was, since she'd billed his ticket to the credit card the club kept on file for his incidental expenses.

Numerous gilded cages hung from the ceiling, all containing at least one person, several containing two. The entertainers moved in time to the music, some holding on to a wire in the top, others grabbing the bars, a few sliding up and down. The atmosphere seethed with energy.

For twenty minutes, he talked to a few people he knew and thanked them for attending and supporting the charity.

Suddenly the lights dimmed. Music shut off, and as if on cue, performers froze in place in their cages.

"Welcome to the Quarter!" The words reverberated through the dungeon, loud and commanding.

On the stage, a flash exploded, and a stunning couple appeared near the edge. They were tall, exceedingly thin, and they looked so much alike he guessed they were twins, though one appeared to be female, the other male.

They were dressed identically in stark-white pantsuits. Each had enormous eyes, with long, feathery lashes. Stunningly, they also sported dark hair, cut in a long bob, accented by angular bangs. Aviana was providing her guests with a spectacle. Despite himself, Mason was intrigued.

The twins clapped in unison, then spoke as one. "Ladies and gentlemen, your seats, please."

Dungeon monitors urged attendees toward the chairs. Mason remained where he was, back pressed against the wall. Tore, Aviana's massive bearded chief dungeon monitor, nodded his permission to allow Mason to stay where he was.

As soon as everyone was in place, the twins spoke again. "Please rise for Mistress Aviana."

The doors were thrown open, and Aviana stalked into the room. Two beautiful male submissives trailed behind her, their leashes attached to her epaulets.

She made her way down the center aisle. With each step,

the gold in her outfit shimmered beneath the spotlights that were turned on her. When she neared the front of the room, Tore fell in step next to her, then offered his hand as she climbed onto her dais.

After waving to acknowledge her adoring crowd, she took her seat on the throne. It had been commissioned years before by an admiring sub, and Aviana's likeness was carved into the top. The rounded arm ends were custom-made from a plaster cast of her grip. As befitting her stature, the upholstery was the finest maroon-colored velvet. It had been crafted with hooks in strategic places where she could attach a slave or submissive.

Once her subs were settled, curled at her feet and chained in place, the twins invited the audience to return to their chairs.

Aviana didn't put on many displays of her dominance, but when she did, the power of her command was as impressive as hell. His gaze strayed to the men at her feet.

At one time, he'd had a submissive who showed him the same kind of deference. But behaving well during a scene hadn't meant a flying fuck outside of it. When she finally left him—at the worst possible time—part of him had been relieved. Since then, he'd avoided personal entanglements.

Until this moment, he hadn't missed having a sub.

Maybe Aviana had been right to encourage him to visit the Quarter more often.

The twins introduced the evening's emcee, Jaxon Mills, a renowned—and at times polarizing—internet marketing superstar. The man had in excess of a million followers on his social media platforms, people who hung on his every video and podcast. He'd started giving speeches to rapt audiences, and since his recent marriage, he'd evidently stepped up his volunteer work as well.

A spotlight hit Jax as he all but leaped onto the stage. He

pointed a finger, then swept it wide, indicating everyone in the crowd. "Get your checkbooks out and your credit cards ready. We have the world's most stunning subs available for you tonight. And it's all for a good cause. You've heard of Reclamation, a charity that benefits seniors living in our great city." On the screens, a video started, showing volunteers scraping paint, hammering shingles into place, installing windows, working on plumbing, replacing furniture and appliances. Everyone was dressed in T-shirts bearing the charity's logo. Volunteers were dirty, sweaty, but smiling, often pictured with the residents they were helping.

Surprising Mason, several of the images included a picture of him.

Without losing a beat, Jaxon continued. "This is what your contribution does. As you know, the need in our community is great. Because of your abundant contributions, last year we restored more than two hundred homes. If you were one of the heroes who made that possible, thank you." He pushed his palms together and bowed. "But let's be honest, shall we?" His voice was low and intimate.

The man's charisma had the room spellbound.

"You know damn good and well that you're fortunate sons of bitches. You can do a fuckpile more than you do. You can dig deeper. If you don't help out tonight, you're a loser, and I'm calling you out on it. We're here for a purpose, and that isn't just to leer at some gorgeous humans. It's to leer *and* make our city proud."

"Hear, hear!" a woman called out.

The video ended, and he stood there in a shimmering pool of light.

When the raucous clapping ended, Jax reached inside his tuxedo jacket, pulled out his wallet, and extracted a check. "Can I get a close-up, please?" Jax held up the piece of paper.

The audience gasped, and Mason nodded approvingly. A

hundred grand. Not a bad way to start the evening. There was a stunning amount of good they could do with that kind of money.

"I have a confession." Jaxon folded the check and used a thumbnail to make the crease sharp. "I'd budgeted fifty thousand for this event. But my wife watched this video. After seeing it, she volunteered for the charity."

A spotlight found a woman who was at the front of the room. She wore a long gold gown, formfitting and glittering with sequins.

"In case you don't know, this is my wife, Willow Mills."

People cheered for her, and Mason knew, firsthand, it was deserved. Despite being a submissive, she was next to her husband, and he credited her with helping him become a better man.

"Tell them what you said to me, honey."

"I told *you* not to be a cheapskate"—a close-up image of her face was being projected on the screen, and her eyes danced with laughter that showed the love between them—"Sir."

The crowd exploded with laughter and more applause.

"All right, all right!" He grinned. When the attendees settled again, he went on. "So I'm passing along her words. Don't be a damn cheapskate. Our seniors have given so much over the years. It's time to give back. And hey, if you're not bidding, or you miss out on your favorite slave, you aren't off the hook."

More hoots and cheers greeted his words.

"There are silent auction items in the bar and reception areas. I know you want to hear some of the highlights. How about a week on a private island in the Caribbean? Griffin Lahey has made the donation, and your stay there includes a chef and an outdoor massage for two." Images scrolled across the screens, of a couple snorkeling among tiny bright-colored fish, then lounging on chairs beneath an umbrella, a cocktail in hand. A sunset was shown next, with kayaks seemingly being rowed out toward it.

How long had it been since Mason had taken a vacation? *Shit.* He dragged his hand through his hair. Not since his dad had passed. The year before that, Mason had been swamped with trying to keep the business running by himself. Maybe that explained his soul-deep exhaustion.

"If that's not your style, how about a high-roller weekend at the Royal Sterling Hotel in Las Vegas?" The resort was pictured, soaring from the Strip with its glass sparkling against the desert sun.

Though Mason wasn't a gambler, the restaurants were legendary, and the pool was the stuff of fantasies. He could sleep there for a week. *Jesus.* He really did need to get away.

"Perhaps you'd like to fall in love with New York this autumn with a package that includes tickets to the hottest performances"—the pictures showed Broadway, then Grand Central Station—"a horse-drawn carriage ride through Central Park, and three nights and unlimited possibilities in the penthouse suite at Le Noble."

Even though he had no one to invite along, Mason was tempted to bid on every damn one of the escapes.

"We have something for every taste. How about a signed giclée by Flahey?"

A few people gasped at the sight of the bold colors and staggering lines slashed across the canvas. Mason knew the artist was well respected. He just didn't understand why. The image was supposed to be of a rock star. If he squinted and turned his head to the side, he could make out a guitar. Maybe. Still, the man commanded a fortune from collectors. The cynic in Mason would definitely prefer that money go to Reclamation.

"If you don't win a weekend with one of the Quarter's

amazing subs or one of our spectacular prizes, we'll still accept your more than generous contribution at the end of the evening. There will be boxes throughout the space, at the coat check, at the exit, and a bunch at the bar. Oh, and one last thing—free drinks for anyone who donates more than five grand." He paused for dramatic effect. "I hope you were prepared for me giving away your booze, Mistress Aviana!"

The camera flashed to her. She gave a half smile and a very regal nod.

"Ah, and finally, anyone who donates over ten thousand dollars will get an exclusive half-day consultation with me."

That was reportedly worth a lot more than ten grand. Jax was gifted at studying a business, branding it, focusing on its strengths, and positioning it for success.

"And if you don't contribute something, your name is going on my shitlist."

His statement was met with laughter—some genuine, some nervous.

"In case this is your first auction, I'll give you a little background on how the evening will proceed. We have a total of fifteen slaves. Yes, fifteen gorgeous, well-behaved individuals"—he looked directly into the camera—"who want to spend the weekend with *you.*"

"Get on with it!" someone shouted.

"They will be presented for your inspection in groups of five. After all the introductions have been made, we will have a brief intermission, and then the bidding will start. Now... who's ready to begin?"

The dungeon plunged into darkness. Moments later, strategic lights hit the stage and the overhead cages with their writhing occupants. Cheers rocked the room, and music again blasted through the air, a thumping, arousing sound that penetrated even Mason's jaded senses.

Behind Jaxon, a black curtain parted to reveal a large

rectangular acrylic platform with two steps leading up to it. There were other round see-through pedestals fanned out in a semicircle.

Jax moved to one side, and Tore strode onto the stage. As usual, he wore a vest. Tonight, however, instead of the customary one with fleur-de-lis, this was crafted from the same brown leather as Mistress Aviana's, and it hung open to show off his honed abs.

Over his shoulder was a long, thick chain, with the first five volunteer slaves attached to it. The group was eclectic. Tall and short. Male and female. Of various ages and ethnicities. Men wore only a scrap of stark-white material, not much more than a pouch that left little to the imagination. The women were dressed in string bikinis beneath sheer sarongs.

The twins floated onto the stage. Together, they unclipped the first slave from the chain and assisted her onto one of the platforms. The camera followed each of her flawless moves.

They repeated the process for each participant. When they were finished, they stepped aside while the camera panned the semicircle. Most of the slaves were relaxed, and one of the men was flexing his biceps, trying to draw attention.

"There you are!" Jaxon called. "It's going to be an extraordinary night!"

Adrenaline fired through the room in the form of claps and appreciative whistles. As much as Mason wanted to be immune, he wasn't. It was a hell of a spectacle.

"Ladies and gentlemen, I present slave number one," Jaxon said when the audience settled down.

The twins helped the first sub from her platform and escorted her to the front of the stage where she stood in the spotlight.

She lowered her gaze, then gave a quick peep through her lashes. It was seductive. Judging by the way one member of the audience sucked in a sharp breath, it was also effective.

"Fiona is looking for a top who is firm but fair. And fortunately for you, she's happy to be won by either a man or a woman." He went on to list her limits and then asked her to turn around so the bidders could study her from every angle. "The minimum bid will be five thousand dollars."

Several people used lights from their cell phones to scribble notes into the margins of their programs. The woman, as beautiful and obviously well trained as she was, didn't stir Mason.

After she'd turned around and presented herself in a variety of poses, the twins returned her to Tore, then escorted the second slave, a man, to the spotlight.

The process was repeated until all the slaves had been introduced. Once they were led away, the next set was brought on. Mason checked his watch. As he'd tried to tell Aviana, this wasn't his kind of event. He either came to scene or he stayed away.

After an interminable amount of time, Tore led the final group in for viewing.

And the woman who was second in line snared his interest.

She was at least half a foot shorter than he was, with impossibly large, wide-open eyes, and brunette hair that tumbled over her shoulders. The gauzy film that covered her couldn't disguise her small beautiful figure. The building's air-conditioning hardened her nipples. To him, she was a tiny wisp of feminine perfection.

Repeating the same process as with the other participants, the twins unclipped her from Tore's chain. As she walked toward her acrylic platform, she missed a step and stumbled slightly. The twins reached for her upper arms to steady her. All the other slaves had appeared to be veterans and enjoying themselves, but her actions betrayed her as a novice.

Mason was torn, his dominant urges stirred. Part of him wanted to protect her. The other, more primal part of his nature urged him to make her his.

What the fuck was wrong with him?

He wasn't given to wild fantasies. Or, maybe he had been, once upon a time. But that had been before Deborah.

The slave gave a quick smile of gratitude before stepping up onto her display platform.

The twins moved aside, and the spotlight moved on to the next contestant. But he looked toward the shadowed part of the stage to watch number twelve. Her shoulders shook, and she curled one hand around the small collar she wore.

He was consumed with a need to know more about her. Why the hell hadn't he accepted one of the programs?

Mason checked his watch again, but for a different reason this time. He was anxious for the pomp and circumstance to be over with so he could have a better look at her.

After the other subs were in place, the first sub was brought forward. His impatience soared. He was interested in only one woman.

Finally, the twins led her to the front of the stage where she stood next to Jax. Her image was projected onto the big screens, making her larger than life. Confounding him, she kept her head lowered, shading her expression.

"Hannah joins us this weekend from Austin, Texas."

When she wobbled a little, Jaxon steadied her, and she grabbed on to him.

Even though he covered his mic to ask if she was all right, the words whispered through the dungeon. "Bend your knees a little. It will help."

She nodded and did what he said.

"Do you want to continue?"

She dropped her hand to her side and nodded several times. "Just nerves."

After Jax studied her for a few seconds, he continued. "Hannah prefers a male Dom who is patient but unyielding. Her limits list includes canes, humiliation, isolation, being shared."

Suited Mason fine. He didn't like to share.

"Let's see your face," Jax encouraged softly, but firmly, part host, part reassuring Dominant.

In the glare of the spotlight, she turned to him, but he nodded toward the audience.

Hannah drew a deep breath before tipping back her chin. Her eyes were unblinking, and a bit wild. They were a rich shade of amber, ringed with a bright gold, speaking of riches. He shook his head. That was a trick of the light and his over-tired imagination.

"Turn around so your potential Doms can inspect you better."

The slave obeyed, and when she faced the front again, she seemed to seek Mason out. That wasn't possible. The lights would prevent her from seeing the back of the room, and the idea of her picking him out from the crowd was ludicrous.

"After the intermission, you'll have the chance to bid on our lovely Hannah. If you're making notes, she's number twelve in your program."

The twins collected her.

Several men grabbed pens. A couple more typed notes into their cell phones, pissing Mason off. *The fuck?* It might be irrational, but Mason decided no Dom but him was spending the weekend with her.

She was his. And within the hour, he intended to claim her.

As if she knew that, she once again glanced in his direction.

The auction continued, but Mason refused to take his gaze or his fantasies from the brunette who'd awakened something inside him that he'd been sure was dead.

CHAPTER 2

When she was unclipped backstage, Hannah propped her shoulders against a brick wall. Now that it was intermission, the entire club buzzed with noise. The music had been turned up again, and the excited slaves were talking to each other—or rather, shouting at each other—to be heard.

But she was drained, as if she'd survived an ordeal.

She'd known she might be nervous, but nothing prepared her for the near paralysis she experienced when the spotlight hit her.

The entire experience was surreal. Because of the glare, the audience was cast in darkness, but the moment she lifted her gaze, a jolt of awareness shot through her. Her intuition shouted that Master Mason Sullivan was out there, looking at her in a contemplative, considering way.

Hannah shook her head to banish the outrageous notion. With his ridiculously handsome looks, broad shoulders, honed biceps, six-pack abs, and haunted soul, he could have his pick of any sub at any time. Behind his back, he was called the One Night Dom. He was known as a considerate top, but he never played with the same submissive more than once. According to her friend, Fiona, a woman had left him so shattered that he offered no commitments and refused to form emotional connections.

Which made him perfect for Hannah since she wanted the escape she only found when scening.

Fiona rushed over, wearing a huge grin. "This is exciting, right?"

Hannah exhaled. How should she respond? In addition to being her best friend, Fiona was the reason Hannah had agreed to participate in the auction.

A couple of weeks ago, Fiona had insisted that Hannah had closed herself off for long enough. The event was for a good cause, and it was really a no-risk situation. Mistress Aviana vetted all members. Hannah would get what she wanted while being safe. As an added precaution, the sub could refuse to go home with the highest bidder—no excuse needed.

"Wait." With a frown, Fiona took Hannah's hands. "Are you okay?

A thrill seeker who enjoyed not knowing what a weekend might hold, Fiona offered herself up every time the club had an auction. "My nerves are shredded," Hannah confessed.

"That can be good. Right? Like exhilarating?"

Maybe, beneath the fear. "It's been a long time."

"I know." Fiona offered a reassuring squeeze.

Ever since the horrible, horrible night with Liam, she hadn't attended a munch or her favorite clubs in Austin. The risk of running into him was too great, and she refused to take the chance.

"If it's too difficult, you don't have to go through with it."

"Slaves!" Tore's commanding voice cut through the chatter.

Obediently, everyone backstage fell silent. Fiona released

Hannah, and the two of them joined the other participants who gathered around Mistress Aviana's most trusted dungeon monitor.

"The intermission will last another twenty minutes. Then I'll lead the first group out. Like before, you'll be unclipped and escorted to a platform. One by one, you'll be called to the front, and you'll be bid on. Then you'll be returned backstage. After the winner has completed the financial requirements, Trinity will come and get you. Any questions?"

"This is the time to drop out if you're going to," Fiona whispered.

As much as Hannah was tempted, a small part of her *was* curious. And damn, she'd missed her connection with the kink world. There was nothing like it. Despite the risk, she wanted to be here. "I want to go through with it." She just wished adrenaline wasn't making her jittery.

"We recommend you spend some time in the club before leaving for the night. Your contract with the winner ends at midnight on Sunday night."

"Will I turn into a pumpkin?" a male sub asked with a giggle.

"Daveed, honey, you're already a pumpkin!" someone called back. "You better hope someone turns you into a princess so someone will buy you!"

"Enough sass." Tore folded his massive arms across his equally impressive chest.

In spite of his gruff demeanor, Hannah would have sworn he cracked a smile. His thick beard made it difficult to be certain.

Tore moved off, and conversation resumed.

"Promise you're not going to pass out on me?" Fiona asked.

A few subs took hold of the massive curtain and drew it back to peek at the audience.

"Oh Lord!" a sub called. "Mistress Mandy is out there! I'd die to have the opportunity to lick her boots."

Noise grew from the makeshift auditorium, turning the energy frenetic and making Hannah's heart race.

"And Master Balderdash!"

A chorus of twitters rippled through the slaves.

"Master Balderdash?" she asked Fiona.

"A good guy, but talks too much, and some of what he says is a little…far-fetched." Fiona shrugged. "Well, complete bullshit, really."

With her luck, Hannah suspected she'd end up with him.

A female submissive dropped the curtain and twirled around. "Fuck! Fuck, fuckity, fuck, fuck!"

"What?" Fiona demanded.

"Master Mason is out there. I thought I saw him. And he was looking at me."

Hannah's stomach plunged into a freefall.

Another sub laughed. "Don't get your hopes up. The One Night Dom can have anyone he wants without paying for the privilege."

Fiona shrugged. "I'd let him put his boots under my bed."

I prefer to be tied to it. Shocked by her thoughts, Hannah again fingered the hated collar.

"Group one, line up," Trinity, the club receptionist, called.

Fiona's eyes brightened. "I'm so excited!"

Fiona hurried over to where Tore stood, holding the long chain. As the twins secured her in place, Fiona rocked back and forth, bouncing a little. So different from Hannah's experience.

The house lights flashed in a subtle signal to let patrons know they needed to return to their seats.

Then Jaxon Mills's seductive voice boomed across the atmosphere. "Ladies and gentlemen, the moment you've been waiting for!"

Ever since Fiona had told her about the megastar, Hannah listened to his audios every day at the gym. He was motivation and inspiration in one kick-ass package. In person, he was even more spectacular. He'd dealt with her nerves in a gentle way that was at odds with his public image.

With a clatter of metal, Tore led the slaves onto the stage.

With her thumb up, Fiona glanced in Hannah's direction. Even with her inner turmoil, Hannah couldn't help but smile at her friend's glee.

Along with a few other participants, Hannah went to peek at the proceedings. Fiona was number one, and Jax called her forward.

Her friend was escorted to the front of the stage. She twirled around like they all had earlier, but this time, Jaxon asked her to strike several different poses, including bending over to ensure she captured the audience's attention.

When he had stretched the anticipation so far that the whoops and hollers bounced from the rafters, Jaxon opened the bidding.

Through it all, he drove up the price, utilizing his customary combination of encouragement and berating. He reminded people of the good their contribution could do in the world, and he challenged them not to be miserly bastards and do something worthwhile.

"Ten thousand dollars," a voice called out, calm and sure.

"Thank you, sir." Jaxon pointed to acknowledge the Dom's bid. "Hit him with the spotlight and show everyone else how it's done!"

The Dom inclined his head when his picture appeared on the big screen.

Hannah didn't recognize the man.

"Master Andrew," one of the slaves standing near her whispered. "He's hot. And unfortunately for me, heterosexual."

She grinned.

"Surely there's someone with deeper pockets, hmm?" Jaxon tossed out the challenge.

A Domme offered ten thousand five hundred. Even though Fiona's head was bowed respectfully, she glanced up to reveal a grin.

"Ten thousand six hundred," the Dom offered.

On and on it went until the Dom won, at twelve thousand nine hundred.

"Thank you, sir!" Jaxon clapped. "And now, I won't be satisfied until we break the thirteen thousand barrier. Next up is slave number two."

Now that Fiona had been auctioned off, Hannah took a moment to scan the guests. She refused to acknowledge that she was looking for Mason, even though her gaze went straight to the spot where he'd been standing.

Not seeing him, she walked away. Nervous energy crawled through her, so she paced, hoping to wear some of it off. A couple of submissives shot her sympathetic glances, and she responded with a wan smile.

"Group two, get ready!" Trinity called. "Master Tore will be back soon!"

Several minutes later, the first five slaves were returned backstage. "We'll get started on the paperwork right away," Trinity promised. "Your name will be called as soon as we're ready for you. Meet me at the podium in the reception area."

The moment the submissives were released from their bondage, Hannah hurried to Fiona. "Who won you?"

"Master Silvestri." She shivered and wrapped her arms around herself. "We played together once, and it was ah-mazing." She rolled her eyes. "Ah-mazing. I was hoping for this." But, ever the good friend, she gave Hannah a quick hug. "Call me tomorrow. I mean it. If you don't, I'll tell Trinity to check up on you."

"Quit worrying."

"No way. This was all my idea, and now I'm feeling a little guilty for talking you into it."

Hannah gave what she hoped was a reassuring nod. "You didn't force me to come here."

They chatted for a few minutes before one of the dungeon monitors came backstage and shouted out Fiona's name.

"This is why I like being first. I'll be having fun while everyone else is still bogged down in the details."

"Fiona!"

"Coming!" Then she grinned. "Have fun, Han. Seriously. This is supposed to be a good time. Remember that, okay? Liam was an asshole. Not everyone is like him." She all but skipped toward the backstage exit.

On some level, Hannah knew her friend was right. But her wounds ran deep.

As the next few slaves were auctioned off, Hannah alternated between watching the proceedings and giving herself a pep talk. She'd meant what she told Fiona. Hannah did want to scene—especially with a Dom she wouldn't run into in her everyday life.

When she signed up, she'd asked to be in the final group so that she would get a sense of how things worked. She hadn't imagined how excruciating the wait would turn out to be. Now she was anxious to get it over with.

Finally, Trinity announced it was time for the remaining slaves to take their places.

As the collar she disliked was clipped into place, Hannah struggled to find peace. Instead, she could barely breathe.

Tore gave them a critical once-over. "Daveed." He pointed to the man right behind Hannah, the one who'd asked if he was going to turn into a pumpkin. She loved his enthusiasm. "Contain yourself, man!"

"Sorry, boss." He sounded anything but. "Excited."

All the other slaves laughed as he adjusted his pouch. Her nerves appreciated the levity.

"Ready, boss."

Tore gave a quick nod of satisfaction. "Hannah," he snapped. "Eyes on me."

"Sorry, Sir."

He gave the chain a massive tug as he led them onto the stage.

This time, Hannah was unclipped and placed on the platform that was in the middle of the semicircle. She was thankful she didn't falter, and she wasn't trembling as hard.

The spotlight was shined on each participant, and the heat made a droplet of sweat trace down between her breasts.

"Ladies and gentlemen, you're running out of time and slaves, as well as the opportunity to do good in our community," Jaxon announced. "Keep in mind, we're all watching you. At the end of the night, you will be a hero or a wannabe. Which are you?"

Laughter rippled through the room, some of it nervous.

"Next up is number eleven. As a reminder, this beauty is looking for a sadist to complement his masochist."

With his incredible skill, Jaxon drove the bidding up to almost twenty thousand dollars before shouting out, "Sold!"

Too soon, the twins came for her.

They each offered a hand as she stepped down from her podium. Hannah paused to take a shaky breath before making her way to the front of the stage.

Even though she knew what to expect, she was hyperaware of her sheer wrap and the string bikini barely covering her. Her image was projected on the big screens, making it impossible for her to hide the way she was twisting her fingers together. Though she'd played at clubs numerous times, she'd never been this exposed.

"This is Hannah's first time on our auction block. You know what that means? I want a premium price for her. Dig deep, gentlemen, because I'm starting the bidding at seven thousand dollars. Who will give it to me?"

She froze, mortified when no one responded.

"Okay," Jaxon said. "You cheap bastards. In that case, bidding is going to start at eight thousand dollars. Who will be first?"

What the hell was he thinking? She bit her bottom lip, wishing she could run away. Suddenly, the event with Liam was looking even less humiliating.

"Eight," a man called.

She exhaled, her shoulders hunching forward.

"Thank you," Jaxon replied. "Who will give me eight five?"

From the right of the room, another man responded.

The music became louder, thumping, adding to the tension as the number went over twelve, then thirteen.

"We have thirteen," Jaxon announced. "Fourteen? It's not often that you have the opportunity to play with someone brand-new. Open your wallets."

"Twenty."

She gasped. The unseen voice was firm with command. Master Mason? More than anything, she wished she could see past the edge of the stage.

"Twenty thousand five hundred."

The bid had come from the opposite side of the room. Hannah wanted to pinch herself.

"Excellent," Jaxon approved, circling her. He pointed to the right side of the spectators. "You're going to give me twenty-one." It was more a statement than a question.

"Twenty-one."

Jaxon played the men off each other until they reached twenty-four.

Then the man on the right calmly said, "Thirty."

Several people in the audience gasped. Hannah's knees wobbled, and the twins raised their hands to steady her.

"Thirty thousand. Thank you. The bid is to you now, Master Kilgore. Thirty-one?"

She sucked in a breath. No response came.

"Going once." He gave a long, dramatic paused. "Twice." He waited even longer.

Her heart thundered.

"Sold! Thank you, Master Mason."

Master Mason? She clasped her hands together on top of her heart. How was this possible? If she could have scripted an evening, it couldn't have been this incredible.

"You may claim your slave at the end of the segment."

As if it were happening outside of herself, Hannah was aware of the twins assisting her back to her podium.

"Congratulations," the slave next to her whispered.

Time slowed as she searched in vain for Master Mason. The One Night Dom. Now that it was becoming more real, a million thoughts crowded her mind. She didn't know much about him. He was devastatingly handsome. But that was hardly the best trait in a Dom. Liam, too, had been gorgeous.

The door to the reception room opened, flooding the threshold with light, enough for her to see the back of a tall man with dark blond hair.

Without a doubt, it was Master Mason.

No one else had that kind of presence.

She pushed out a hot, anxious breath. Was he lenient? Fair? Demanding? Would his touch be gentle or harsh? What kinks did he have?

God. She could no longer tell where one thought ended and the next began.

The rest of the auction dragged on for another thirty agonizing minutes.

When they were backstage, Daveed grabbed her up in a big hug. "Oh, Hannah, baby! You are so lucky. One Night Dom is dishy." He batted his false eyelashes. "I wish I were you." He gave her a quick kiss on the cheek. "Do all the things. *All* the things."

"Daveed!" Trinity shouted.

Tore and the twins left to help reset the dungeon with the equipment that had been stowed away.

Tension turned her tummy into knots when a dungeon monitor called the name of another slave, leaving just Hannah and two others backstage. Again, she regretted asking to be in the final group.

She paced to the far end of the area, and when she turned back, *he* stood there in his black tailored tuxedo, with his legs spread wide and his arms folded. Hoping to appear confident, she paused. But then she betrayed herself by grabbing hold of the sarong that was knotted at her shoulder.

Master Mason pointed to a spot in front of him as if he didn't doubt—even for a moment—that she would obey. "Come here." His tone was rich and firm, turning her insides into a river of compliance.

Her pulse hammered, drowning out the noise around them. Power emanated from him, drawing her toward him. A now familiar instinct to save herself urged her to walk a little slower, stay outside his force field.

Hannah stopped precisely where he had indicated.

The scent of his alpha male pheromones stamped the air, and her.

"I couldn't wait to meet you."

Hannah tipped her head back to meet his shadowed, haunted eyes. Then she wished she hadn't. If she'd lowered her head, she wouldn't have seen the pain written in the jade-colored depths, wouldn't have had an urge to heal him flicker through her.

No doubt she wasn't the first woman, sub, to be tempted by that ridiculous thought.

This was a weekend. Nothing more.

"What should I call you?"

His voice was hypnotic. Steel and silk. For a moment, she considered using a scene name, but she'd had too many lies told to her in the past. "Hannah." Then because she was trusting him with her safety, she opted to share her full name. "Hannah Gill." Then, belatedly, she added, "Sir."

His lips curled in a small, slight smile. It didn't make him appear any less formidable. "Sir is fine. Mr. Sullivan. Mason."

"Master?"

He shook his head and moved his hand toward the leather cinched around her throat. "May I touch you?"

Unable to find her voice, she nodded.

"Master is a much more formal term. Something"—he traced the buckle—"much more permanent. It speaks of commitment, doesn't it? Responsibility. A person who is honorable."

"Which you're not?"

"It depends on your point of view, I suppose. What you consider honorable. Where's the line between duty to your sub and duty to someone you love?" He skimmed his finger lower. The moment his hot, rough skin touched hers, awareness shot through her, scattering her thoughts and leaving raw need in its terrible wake. "But I take care of the women who submit to me." He pressed against the hollow of her throat. "I offer nothing more."

"I understand…Mason."

"Good." He nodded.

He was warning her not to get attached. No expectations.

One Night Dom. The earlier words and giggles from the slaves ricocheted through her mind.

Trinity peeked around the corner. “Master Mason!”

With a smile, he pulled his hand back in achingly slow measurements, and Hannah’s skin instantly cooled.

“We have a few details to handle.”

Money. Thirty thousand dollars. The sum was beyond her wildest dreams, enough to pay off the note on her car and some of her credit card debt. And he’d offered it for a couple of nights with her.

“Because you’ve never met me before, I suggest we spend some time here, getting to know each other a bit. Then, if you’re willing, we can make use of a private room on the second floor, giving you a chance to be sure you want to leave with me.”

Mistress Aviana had strict rules for what happened in the main dungeon and the quieter, more secluded area tucked behind it. But upstairs, almost anything was permitted, including nudity and sexual contact. The club’s safe word still applied, and the scenes were monitored.

“What do you say?”

“Yes.”

“I’ll see you up front when the formalities are handled.” He brushed hair back from her forehead, and his touch was achingly gentle.

For a moment, she was tempted to wrap her hand around his, but that would imply a familiarity they didn’t enjoy.

He followed Trinity from the space, and Hannah couldn’t take her gaze from him.

Daveed hurried over. “That man is a honeypot. I’d like to dip my fingers in him.”

She laughed, and it was then that she realized she’d been holding her breath.

"Girl, enjoy your weekend, but don't get your heart all wrapped up in that broken mess."

"I won't." She wondered which one of them she was reassuring.

It was less than ten minutes until Trinity returned. "Ready?"

The same instinct that assailed her earlier flashed through Hannah's brain again. Red. Danger. Not physically. Her body was safe in his hands, but her emotions? He overwhelmed her senses. Yet, as if compelled, she ignored her internal warning system and followed Trinity to the reception room.

On a side table, a slave was signing a piece of paper, and her temporary owner stood next to her.

Mistress Aviana stood behind the podium, flanked by two gorgeous—and mostly naked—young blond men on all fours.

Aviana gestured for Hannah to approach.

Master Mason was in the corner, talking with Jaxon. The moment Mason noticed her, he excused himself and walked toward her.

"Be gone," Aviana said, waving him away. With a scowl, she added, "And this time follow the damn rules before I have you thrown out."

"Of course, Milady." He inclined his head, but his smile betrayed him. He charted his own course.

"He thinks he can get away with murder," Mistress Aviana said when he returned to Jaxon's side. She leaned forward conspiratorially. "The truth is, with the right people, he can. Which is why I wanted to speak with you alone. Despite his generous bid, you are not obligated to anything. The choice is entirely yours."

Hannah risked a glance his direction…to find him watching her. Excitement and fear slammed together in a potent combination. He'd brought arousal to life for the first time in years.

"Hannah?"

"Sorry." She turned back to the club's owner.

"Would you like to proceed?"

Whatever the weekend held, Hannah wanted the experience. "Yes, Milady."

CHAPTER 3

Mistress Aviana signaled for Mason. "If you'll excuse me," he said to Jax, anxious to make his escape and claim Hannah.

"I'm going to invite you to all the fundraisers I emcee for. You make me look good."

"Check your ego," Mason told his longtime friend with a grin. "Had nothing to do with your skills. I would have paid anything for the weekend with Hannah." He looked over at her again. She was still clutching the sarong tightly. But if he had his way, the material and everything else hiding her would be lying on the floor in the next ten minutes.

"I know how it is."

Mason had never seen a man so besotted with his wife. The cynic in him no longer believed in happily ever after. Love sometimes meant being selfless. He'd never met a woman capable of it.

"Enjoy your weekend," Jaxon said.

Mason fully intended to.

"Let's get the formalities out of the way, shall we?" Aviana began when he joined her.

"The sooner the better." Time was ticking.

"Hannah, do you consent to spend the weekend with Master Mason? Please know that while you're at the Quarter, the word *red* will end any scene, trumping the agreement you're about to sign."

He rocked back onto his heels in a mostly useless attempt to rein in his mounting impatience.

Hannah nodded. And that soothed his inner beast. For the moment.

"If at any time you wish to end the weekend, please call the number on your agreement. One of our monitors will fetch you, day or night. Your safety and well-being are of utmost importance to me."

"Can we hurry this up?" he demanded.

"No, Master Mason, we can't." The club owner didn't even glance in his direction.

While he appreciated Aviana's concern, there was no way Hannah would want to end the weekend early. He'd make sure of it. "She's safe with me."

"To reiterate, your limits include"—Aviana glanced up and shot Mason a look that warned him to remain silent —"canes, humiliation, isolation, being shared. Is there anything else you'd like to add, Hannah?"

"No breaking the skin or permanent marks, Milady."

Which I would never do with a weekend sub.

As Aviana added to her list, he swept his gaze over Hannah's slender body. He'd never been tempted to pierce or tattoo a sub. Maybe because it was suddenly taboo the idea intrigued him. Perhaps something subtle, in a place only he knew about?

"Nothing else, Hannah?"

"No, ma'am."

"In that case, I need you both to see Trinity. She'll print out your forms, and you'll both need to sign them and acknowledge receipt. Then you can get on with your evening."

"I'll want a private room in about half an hour."

Aviana raised one of her carefully crafted eyebrows. "Hannah?"

"Yes, Milady. I'd like that too."

While Mason drummed his fingers on the table, Aviana scanned a computer in front of her. "Room seven will be available."

He nodded. Then, unable to contain the primal possession that thumped into him, he placed his fingers in the small of Hannah's back.

Her body trembled, and his dick hardened. He liked her being nervous, and he intended to exploit that until he was her whole world.

It took Trinity less than two minutes to process their paperwork. After they'd both affixed their signatures to the bottom of the pages and accepted their copies, he folded the papers and tucked them inside his tuxedo jacket and then escorted Hannah to the cloakroom.

Since he hadn't shown up intending to bid or even play with a sub, he hadn't brought his toy bag. Fortunately, a couple of vendors were in attendance, offering all kinds of fetish toys and clothing, including a woman who made exquisite chain mail. "Let's have a look, shall we?" he asked Hannah.

They wandered to the first table, and he picked up a heavy black flogger with thick strands. Since she was so small, they would wrap around her body, allowing him to cover a lot of her with each stroke.

He offered it to her.

"Sir?" She didn't reach for the handle as he expected.

"What do you think of it?"

"I think it's an unfair question. What if I think it's too

much? Not enough? Does my opinion matter? Isn't it for you to choose?"

"I like it. But before I spend that kind of money"—it wasn't a lot for something so well crafted, but if it was going to hang forgotten in his armoire, he'd rather select something else—"I want to be sure it intrigues you."

She accepted it then. "It's heavy." She fingered the falls, then lifted it up in front of her face. "I like the way it smells."

"An aphrodisiac."

"Maybe."

The black was sexy next to her pale skin. "Are you wondering what it will feel like?"

She met his gaze. This close, her amber eyes were startling, and easy to read. But he wanted her to say the words.

"I can imagine it taking my breath away."

"It might."

"If it pleases you, then yes." She offered it back to him.

He let the craftsman know they would take it. "What else do you like, Hannah?"

"That's quite enough, Sir."

Under ordinary circumstance, he might agree. But he intended to make this weekend memorable for her. "Canes are on your limits list." He took her hand and led her beyond them. "Paddles?"

Her mouth parted, and he wasn't sure whether it was with delight or fear.

"I tried Lexan, and it was a little extreme."

"Wood? Leather?" There were numerous options from something fun to something harsh.

She looked at a number of items, then fingered a thick wooden one, glossy enough to gleam in the overhead light.

"It could deliver a hell of a wallop." And make a very satisfying thud.

Hannah swallowed hard.

For a moment, Mason considered buying it but then changed his mind. She should have one, but he intended to make it himself.

"I just finished up some of these dragon tails." The craftsman selected one and handed it across to Mason.

This he liked. The handle was braided red and black leather, and it was a beautiful piece. "What do you think?"

"It's pretty."

He grinned. That wasn't generally how he made decisions about BDSM toys, but it worked. Mason signaled to the vendor. "We'll take it."

"Sir! This is all so extravagant."

At home, in his armoire, he had plenty of implements, but it had been a lot of years since he'd had the opportunity to purchase something for a specific woman. He'd missed it.

"Anything else for you this evening?" the craftsman asked.

"No. Thank you." Then Mason changed his mind. "A smaller flogger, perhaps."

"Sir," Hannah protested. "This is all too much."

"Any specific type?" the vendor asked.

"Something soft. Suede, perhaps." Something he could use for a prolonged scene.

"You're in luck." The man reached below the table and pulled out a velvet-lined tray with six different options. "One of my associates has started making them."

At the sight of the floggers, Hannah whispered, "Wow." Rather than the expected red and black, or even purple, these were pastels, pinks and baby blues. One was white, reminding him of the bikini she wore.

He picked it up and made a figure-eight motion with it. She didn't look away while he tested the grip. It was certainly big enough, maybe ten inches. The fronds were about eighteen inches long, and they were nice and wide. "Do you like it?"

"Yes."

"Because it's pretty?"

She smiled. And that was reason enough for him to buy it.

"It looks fun," she said. "Not too harsh. I used to have one similar."

"That will do it," Mason told the vendor. "Unless you have any bags?"

The man nodded. "Anything else? Lube? Condoms?"

Mason had one in his wallet, of course, but they hadn't discussed having sex. He hadn't fucked anyone in close to a year. But he couldn't imagine not having her. He wanted her on his cock, beneath him, in front of him. He wanted to explore every one of her nuances "Hannah?"

"Perhaps Sir might want to be prepared."

Christ almighty. His cock was ready to burst out of his slacks. "Add a box to the bill."

The vendor keyed all the information into his electronic pad, then handed over the device for Mason's credit card.

Gently, Hannah placed her fingers on his wrist. "Are you sure you want to do this?"

Even more so now.

Once he had signed the screen and the toys were stowed in the bag, the vendor offered his business card. "Pleasure, sir. Thank you."

Mason slung the bag over his shoulder. "Would you like to join me at the bar?" At least the glassed-in area would be marginally quieter than the rest of the dungeon.

"Sounds good."

Near the frosted glass door leading into the dungeon, Hannah hesitated. "Uh, I'm unsure of the protocol you'd like, Sir."

Meaning, should she precede him, or perhaps trail behind? "Thank you for asking. Walk next to me until we have the chance to talk."

He opened the door. Thunderous music blasted the dungeon. Couples and moresomes hung around, talking, and there were lines in front of all the equipment. The dancers still writhed in cages, and Xander—a renowned rigger—was artfully suspending a woman on the stage. A hired professional photographer was snapping pictures of her.

Since Hannah's steps were slow, he reached for her hand and found it fisted at her side. "Relax," he said against her ear. "I've got you."

She nodded.

He led her to the bar that was decorated with over-the-top Louisiana paraphernalia, an LSU pennant, Mardi Gras beads and masks, a New Orleans Saints football helmet, signed football jerseys, a trumpet, even framed line drawings of buildings in the French Quarter. Unsurprisingly, most of the area was filled with couples like them, getting to know each other. The long bar was occupied with singles watching the happenings on the dungeon floor.

As they passed a small booth, Daveed waved at Hannah.

"A friend of yours?" Mason asked.

"You could say that. He kind of took me under his wing so I wasn't as nervous. Don't tell him I said so, but I think he has a crush on you."

"Is that right?" He raised an eyebrow. "I had no idea."

Mason found them a table in a corner. A tented card was decorated with carnival masks and featured the evening's specialties.

Hannah picked up the menu and looked it over. "Oh, heaven in a glass. They have a brandy milk punch. Named the Fister." She grinned and gave a mock shiver. "Can you believe that?"

"Sounds wicked." And it gave him ideas.

"Doesn't it? Okay, and the Golden Gin Fizz. It's made with heavy cream, lemon juice, simple syrup, and orange flower water. Oh, and egg white." She showed him the picture. "They call it rich and sinful." She wrinkled her nose. "I'm not sure whether the egg white makes it healthy or not."

"We can go with that. Health food."

"Like a smoothie. Only better."

But they wouldn't be having alcoholic beverages this evening, unless she wanted one later. Aviana had a strict no-drinking-while-scening rule. Members who imbibed had their hand marked, and dungeon monitors watched closely to be sure no one attempted to skirt her regulations.

Jaxon and Willow entered the area, and they were greeted warmly as they walked through the space.

When Jax saw Mason, he headed toward them.

Mason stood.

"Once she knew you were here, Willow wanted to say hello."

He reached his hand toward Hannah, and she accepted it. He drew her up and toward him. "Hannah, you've met Jaxon."

She smiled at him. "Thank you for being so kind up there on the stage."

"Happy to help. Love it when people face their fears and trounce them into the ground."

Mason then introduced Hannah to Jax's wife. "This is Willow, a woman of extraordinary patience."

Jax shrugged. "Still can't believe she puts up with me."

"I would never have your kind of courage," Willow gushed, hugging Hannah. "I'd have passed out for sure."

"Remember," Jaxon went on, "you've earned a consultation with me because of your contribution."

"Stuck in the typical conundrum." Mason shrugged. "We're turning down business right now because we don't have enough help. If I hire more help, I'm not sure I can grow the business fast enough to afford the additional overhead."

"Worth having a look at."

"I'll give you a call." Mason nodded. "Would you like to join us?"

Jaxon opened his mouth to reply, but Willow squeezed his arm. "I think they might want some time alone."

"Your wife is correct." Mason grinned. "I was being polite."

"I can take a hint," Jax said, straightening his bowtie as he glanced at Hannah. "You're a lucky man, Mason." Then he covered Willow's hand with his own. "I wish you as much happiness as I've found."

"So down to earth," Hannah said when they returned to their seats. "He wasn't what I expected. Compassionate."

"Don't let that get out." Mason grinned.

"They seem so much in love."

He'd seen them enough to know it wasn't an act. Jax was genuine when he said marrying Willow had been good for him.

When the server arrived, Hannah ordered a diet soda while he opted for a sweet tea. He added a bottled water to the tab, so that he'd have it for her when the scene ended.

Once their drinks were in front of them, he propped an ankle on his opposite knee and regarded her. "What are you hoping to get out of this weekend?"

"Fun," she admitted, stirring her straw absently. "It's been…" She hesitated. "A really long time since I've scened. I stayed away…"

"Go on. You're safe with me. I won't repeat anything you say."

Still, she hesitated before speaking again. "I wanted to be sure I was over him, you know?"

"Him?"

She scooted back in her chair, putting a little more distance between them. "A Dom. We were…" She seemed to choose, then reject certain words. "Involved. The relationship lasted a little more than a year. And I didn't want to just jump into something else. I took some time to figure out who I was and what I wanted."

He frowned. "And you've done that?"

"Enough to know that I'm not looking for anything permanent. So a weekend appealed to me."

"In his introduction, Jax said you're from Austin. As in you live there?"

"Yes. I travel to New Orleans a few times a year. My best friend lives here. Fiona." She released her straw, but it continued to make a slow circle. "You might know her?"

"I do."

"Anyway, she talked me in to doing this."

"Look, Hannah—"

She reached across the table to put her hand on top of his. "Don't get me wrong, please. I'm consenting, and I want to do this. Very much."

Her silence lasted so long, Mason wondered if there was something else she wanted to say.

"There's no real risk, right? We are going to enjoy a couple of days together, then I travel back to Austin and return to my regular life. You get to do the same."

Why the hell did that idea make him so damn uncomfortable? It should be the perfect arrangement.

"About the condoms?" She moved her hand away. "Sex."

"I have no expectations." *Desires, yes. Rampant.* "We don't have to do anything you don't want to."

"I'm not looking for it." She shifted her weight. "But if it happens, I'm fine with it. I mean, as long as we're safe."

"Agreed."

She pushed aside her drink. "You didn't pay thirty thousand dollars to talk to me."

"On the contrary. I'm enjoying this very much." The

admission surprised him. He hadn't dated since Deborah, which meant he hadn't indulged in much casual conversation. Business lunches were plenty, but getting to know a woman was unusual.

"So maybe it's me who is impatient," she admitted.

He stood and offered his hand. "I never like to keep a lady waiting."

Mason guided her from the bar and toward the door that led into the private area, built in a horseshoe shape around the main dungeon. Tonight, it was much more crowded than usual, and the main difference between it and the dungeon was that the music wasn't as loud.

He continued to the stairs, and when they reached the landing, he asked her to join him at the wrought-iron railing. "I have your list of limits. Now I'm interested in learning what you want so that I can ensure you have *fun* this weekend."

From here, there was an unobstructed view of the main dungeon, and the U-shaped area that framed it. To one side was Rue Sensuelle, or as members called it, Kinky Avenue. There, Mistress Aviana had devoted an entire section of the club to partitioned-off areas that appealed to various role-play fantasies. There was a schoolroom, a pair of stocks, a Victorian bedchamber, even a corporate boardroom. This evening, by way of something new, there was also a police interrogation room. But his temporary submissive was fixated on the doctor's office. As they watched, one of the slaves who'd been auctioned off was having her right foot placed into a stirrup.

Hannah shivered.

"Was that a good shiver? Or did you bump up against a limit?"

"It's more..." With her free hand, she played with the knot of her sarong. "I don't know. So intimate."

"Like having your Dom insert a butt plug, for example?"

Mouth wide, she looked at him. But she didn't say no.

"Ass play is okay with you, Hannah?"

"Yes, Sir."

Fuck.

Until now, he'd never considered attaching a submissive to a table. Now he was contemplating making one just for her.

The Dom slid back a piece of the table, leaving the woman's buttocks suspended with nothing beneath it.

Hannah clenched his hand tight.

The man leaned over his sub, kissed her, and tucked a finger inside her bikini bottom.

"Oh, God," Hannah whispered.

"Do you like that? The way he's exploring her? And she's helpless? She can't get away, can she? No matter how far he might split her apart, with his fingers, maybe a toy."

Hannah's gaze never left the scene, but her breaths shortened.

The Dom picked up a roll of purple tape, then reached inside the bikini top to cover her nipples, in accordance with club rules. Then, he handcuffed her wrists above her head. Only then did he pull out a pair of safety scissors to cut off the virginal-looking white material.

Her large breasts spilled free, and he cupped them, teased them, seeming to measure them.

"Would you like that, Hannah? Having me manhandle you? Exploring all your body's secrets?"

"I..." She swallowed hard, then looked at him.

It was tantamount to a confession, and he savored it.

Before they left, they watched a naughty schoolgirl climb up onto a chair and lean against the chalkboard to get her calves smacked with a ruler.

Though she was intrigued, his patience neared an end. He was greedy to be alone with Hannah. "Shall we?"

After a final look over her shoulder at the doctor's office scene, she nodded. "Yes, Sir."

So compliant. "What intrigued you most?" he asked as they climbed the stairs.

"Honestly? Everything."

Maybe she wasn't as innocent as he'd believed, and that captivated him all the more.

They checked in with the monitor for the private rooms. Once they were sealed inside, all the noises from the club vanished.

He was alone with his sexy, nervous sub. Was there anything more appealing than the thrill of being with someone brand-new? "Please stand in the center of the room and remove your shoes." While the heels did lewd things to his libido, he wanted her aware of her submissiveness. And the fact that she'd found the examination table intriguing gave him some insights as to how he should proceed.

He carried the bag to the metal table against one wall. "Tell me about your limits around humiliation."

"Mostly, I don't want other people witnessing things that might be embarrassing."

She bent to remove her first shoe.

"Scening in general?"

"It's a little complicated for me. I do like going to a club, but things that are outside my comfort zone are really difficult. If we're alone, I'm okay."

"Give me some examples."

"Tethering." She spoke softly. "Being caged. Things where I'm ignored, left alone." She paused. "Abandoned."

His breath constricted.

"And I'm not comfortable wearing a collar."

He frowned. Honestly, this was the first sub he'd heard

that from. In his past, his submissives had been upset when he'd denied them a collar. "You don't like the one you have on?" It was club-issued, with a fleur-de-lis stamped into the soft leather.

"I hate it."

Immediately, he crossed to her to unfasten it. "Lift your hair." Because she still wore one shoe, her angle was slightly awkward, but he removed the collar in a matter of seconds. The metal buckle hit the wooden floor with a clatter.

"Thank you." She exhaled.

Perplexed, he frowned. "Why did you allow the Quarter to place it on you if it's a limit?"

"How would it have looked if all the other participants had one on, and I didn't?" She shrugged, a delicate little move. "And it didn't really mean anything. It was part of the show, Tore leading us all in together. There was no commitment. More like a prop in a play."

"It's the commitment that bothers you? The symbol of a Dom's possession?"

"Yes." She stroked her neck where the leather had snuggled her skin. "Once was enough for me."

Until now, her voice had been soft, but her confession was roughened by emotion and conviction.

"Do you want to tell me about it?"

"No." She blinked. "I mean, no, Sir. I'd rather not."

He continued to study her, the layer of emotion in her eyes. He wanted to push, learn more about her.

"That's why I'm here."

"Anonymity? Lack of commitment?"

"That sounds..." She worried her lower lip. "I guess I wouldn't put it that way."

"But?"

"Maybe you're right. It sounds harsh, though."

"It wasn't a judgment call. Especially from me."

"You have demons of your own, Sir? Scars, maybe?"

"You could say that."

They only had the weekend together, and she owed him nothing, no deep confessions, not even transparency.

"I gave away some of my power to someone who didn't deserve it. I'm not interested in doing that again."

He nodded. She'd admitted a lot more than he had, and yet it only made him want to dig deeper until he uncovered all her secrets. Respecting the boundary she'd erected, he asked, "Is there anything specific I need to know?"

"No. I'll be honest with you if I'm uncomfortable about something."

"What is your safe word?"

"I'll stick with the same one as the club. Red. Yellow for slow."

Mason nodded. "Please remove your other shoe." He offered his arm for support, and the way she delicately placed fingers on him gave him a distinct thrill.

When she was barefoot, she straightened her body.

She was so small that an unanticipated urge to wrap her in his arms and protect her from the world's evils slammed into him. *What the fuck?* He wasn't a knight in shining armor. He shook his head. Not ever again, and he was annoyed as hell at himself for even entertaining the notion.

"Sir?"

Aware that he was grinding his back teeth, he shoved his thoughts away. "Help me off with my jacket, Hannah." Dominance was natural for him, and he moved toward its familiarity.

As competent as any man's valet, she held the material while he shrugged it off. "Good. Now hang it on the back of the chair."

Her steps were silent, but her breaths weren't. He was being a jerk. There was no need to order her around like that. But at that moment, it was better than revealing that he'd experienced a flash of emotion that momentarily left him vulnerable.

He faced her again when she returned to the center of the room. This time, he used a gentler tone. "And now my cufflinks, if you will?"

"Of course, Mason." With shaky hands, she did as he said. "That's an interesting symbol on them. An owl?"

"Yes."

"From Greek mythology? Athena's owl."

"You're well studied." Another thing he appreciated about her.

"I was in a sorority."

"That explains it."

She closed her hand around the pieces of metal.

"Put them on the table," he instructed.

"Yes, Sir." Even though her words were a whisper, they reverberated in the silence.

He'd heard those words numerous times, but until now, they'd never meant anything to him. She genuinely wished to please him.

He studied her as she crossed to the table, watching her legs flex, her hips sway. Mason scened often enough. But somewhere along the line, he'd allowed his experiences to leave him jaded. It had been a long time since he'd savored every moment of being with a submissive.

Her steps silent, she returned to him.

"Now roll back my shirtsleeves."

She looked up at him and licked her lower lip. It would be less intimate and more expedient for him to do it himself, but he wanted her touch. She turned back the first cuff and smoothed it before continuing. "You know why we're doing this, sub?"

"So you're more comfortable?" She didn't look up from her task.

"No."

"Sir?" She finished rolling the first sleeve into place before meeting his gaze.

"So that I don't get wet from your juices while I inspect you. Your breasts, your pussy. You're going to like that, aren't you?"

She dug her nails into him.

"You might want to let go, little one." He grinned.

"Oh." Instantly she released him. "I'm sorry."

He wasn't. He enjoyed unnerving her. "Do you need to be reminded what my command was?"

"Sir! No. I'm sorry."

"No apology needed. I don't mind spanking you for your lapses."

Her hand hovered over his arm.

"That's not on a limits list?"

"Spanking?" She studied him with a slight smile. "Not at all."

The intimacy of it, he guessed. Really, there was nothing much more personal than a hand on bare skin. She wouldn't be alone or abandoned that way. "If you could only choose one method of impact play, what would it be?"

"Flogging."

Which was a good thing since he was now the proud owner of two new ones.

Her breaths turned shallow. "There's nothing better."

"When we were shopping, we never discussed a single tail?"

She hadn't managed to roll back his second cuff. "I've never experienced that. It's scary, but I might be willing."

It was something he only did in a long-term relationship

or with a sub he knew was experienced, so why had he even asked the question? "Of course. How about a crop?"

At his rapid change of conversation, she blinked. "Yes."

"You had that same kind of enthusiasm when you talked about the brandy milk punch."

"They called it the Fister, Sir."

He angled his head to one side. "Was that a hint? Suggestion?"

Twin scarlet flames painted her cheeks. "I'm not sure I'm that brave. I was, ah…talking about the drink."

Were you? Were you indeed? "Tawse?"

"I've always wanted to try that. I'm not really into pain all that much, but I like impact play."

"When you have fantasies, are they about impact play?"

"Almost always. Yes."

"I'm interested in discovering your thresholds. Since you've yet to roll up my right shirtsleeve, perhaps we should begin with eight spanks?"

Her hands fell to her sides. "You're distracting, Sir."

He was absolutely delighted with her, in her. "Are you blaming me for your transgressions, sub?"

Hannah shook her head. "Of course not. No, Sir." Right away, she reached for his arm to roll up the sleeve.

Because he liked her touch, he let her finish her task. "Stand up straight." Once she had, he captured her chin. "Where shall I start my very thorough investigation of all your secrets?"

She gasped. This time, he knew her better. She was nervous, but not alarmed. He used the tip of his middle finger to trace one of her eyebrows. Then, he stroked across a cheekbone before brushing hair back from her face.

Hannah scarcely breathed.

With his thumbnail, he feathered a touch across her lips.

In silent, sensual invitation, she parted them slightly. "That's right. Wider."

Trembling, she opened her mouth for him. Gently, he inserted a finger inside her warmth, and she waited for his command before cradling him with her tongue and sucking. "Very attentive."

Mason pulled out his finger and outlined her ear before tugging gently on the lobe. With a tiny moan, she turned into him. She might love impact play, but she responded beautifully to any kind of touch. Being this gentle with a sub was a new experience for him, and he was surprised by how much he enjoyed it.

He grabbed a handful of her sarong. "I'm going to take it off you." It hadn't provided her with any modesty, but undressing her was symbolic.

"Yes, Sir."

His motions deft, he worked the knot loose. Next, he tugged the gauzy material from her, leaving her in front of him wearing just the white bikini. "You are beautiful, Hannah."

"When you say it—" She stopped herself. "Thank you."

Mason carried the sarong to the table and laid it alongside his cufflinks. Then he grabbed a chair from the corner and placed it about four feet in front of her. "Wondering what I'm up to?" He took his seat.

Her gaze was riveted on him.

"Spread your legs, please."

Slowly, she did as he asked.

"Is your pussy wet for me, Hannah?"

"Sir—"

"Just answer the question. Are you wet for me?"

"Yes." There was no apology in her whisper, just a beautiful confession.

"You have no idea how happy that makes me. Now put

two fingers inside yourself—don't play with yourself, because you certainly do not have permission to do that—then hold up your hand for inspection."

She closed her eyes.

"No. No hiding from me. I want to see your expressions. So much so that I might add blindfolds to my limits list and never permit you the anonymity."

Either because she wanted to be submissive or because it was another way to hide, she lowered her gaze as she dipped her fingers into her pussy.

Maybe later, he'd have her masturbate for him. If he could tolerate watching without touching. "That's it. Now take them out and come here." He spread his legs, and she closed the distance between them to stand between his thighs. "Hold your hand up to the light." Moisture glittered on her fingers. "Do you see that? Proof of how much your body wants me?"

"Yes," she whispered.

"Now put them in my mouth."

Her breath whooshed out in a frantic burst. But damn, she was so perfect, never hesitating.

It had been a long time since he'd had an experience with a woman that was remotely like this. He visited the Quarter and played with willing women in the public areas. He flogged them, perhaps used a paddle or a single tail, and he was sure they were satisfied with the experience. But with her, perhaps because of her honesty or the vulnerabilities she'd admitted to, he was taking his time, exploring the emotional angles as well as the physical ones.

He closed his mouth and sucked, softly at first, then harder, communicating how this evening—and the rest of the weekend—was going to go.

"Mason..." She moaned and leaned into him.

Her taste was tangy—passion and submission—nectar of

the gods. All of it was for him, because of him. The realization was a drug he couldn't get enough of.

Slowly, he released her. "I will savor your juices every day, little sub." He placed his hands on her hips—so fucking dangerous to his restraint—and eased her back a couple of steps. "Now return to where you were standing and remove your top." If he took the damn stringy thing off her, he might fuck her where she stood. And there was a long way to go before either of them were ready for that.

For a few seconds, she fumbled with the clasp behind her. Giving up, she moved on to the knot at her nape. With any other sub, he'd offer to help. But the way she wiggled and contorted her body appealed to his baser nature.

The material fell, partially covering one of her nipples but leaving the other exposed. The peaks were thick and hard against the dusky pink halo of her areolas. "I could look at you all night and never grow tired."

She turned the bikini top so that the clasp was in the front, then parted it and allowed the top to fall to the floor.

"I'm looking forward to inspecting every inch of you. Please put your hands behind your neck."

Her chest heaving, she complied with his command.

"Perfect." He stood and circled her, taking her in from every angle, appreciating her curves.

Since she went rigid, perhaps in anticipation of his touch, he returned to his chair. She expelled a small breath, with what sounded like frustration. *Good.* "Now remove your bikini bottom."

"Yes, Sir," she whispered, the words so soft they hovered on the air.

There was nothing seductive in her motions. She was a woman trying to please her man, and quickly. He liked that.

Her pubic area was smooth, no doubt waxed. "Brazilian?"

"Yes, Sir."

"Perhaps you should show me. I'll be certain your technician did a good job."

"You..." She blinked at him.

"Come here, then face away from me. Bend over, spread your legs as wide as you can, then hold your ass cheeks apart."

Her cheeks flushed. Still, she walked to him, her eyes remaining locked on him.

"Another step closer, Hannah." It took all his resolve not to reach for her full, beautiful breasts.

Without prompting, she turned away from him, then bent over. She reached back to hold her buttocks apart.

"Wider."

She made a little sound of protest but complied.

"You are so beautiful when you're spread for me." He stood and feathered three fingers over her pubic area. "So smooth." He stroked between her labia, and she rose up. "Keep your feet flat on the floor, sub. We'll do this at my pace."

"Yes, Sir," she mumbled.

Mason pressed his thumb against her clit.

"Argh!"

He grinned. "Are you horny?"

"Oh, Sir!"

"What am I doing, Hannah?"

"Playing with me, Sir?"

"Inspecting," he corrected. "This is about me, not you. I'm learning. You're submitting. So you're not going to come, are you?" As he spoke, he continued to slide his fingers between her slick pussy lips.

Her legs trembled.

"I asked you a question."

"No, Sir."

"You seem to like the way I inspect you."

Rather than saying anything, she groaned.

"Keep your hands in place. I like the sight of your cunt and ass. In fact, spread even farther, please."

"Oh, Sir. I'm not sure that's possible." Her skin took on a slight glow from her efforts and the struggle to stay in position.

"I'm quite sure you'll manage." To ensure she did, he helped her along, placing his hands on top of hers and forcing her buttocks apart. "Now all you need to do is stay in this position."

She was beautifully exposed to him. "I'm going to see for myself how wet you are."

"Please, yes."

Keeping his thumb on her clit, he entered her with one finger, then a second. Her pussy convulsed around him as she struggled to hold off a climax. So damn hot. He sought her G-spot, then pressed against it.

"Oh, God!" She dropped her hands to her knees.

"My instructions were explicit, Hannah. You weren't given permission to break your pose."

"But—"

"This inspection is not over." Relentlessly, he edged her. Her responses were so honest. This was Dom and sub the way it was meant to be, no artifice. "Show me your ass, Hannah."

She reached back, only to drop her hands again when he pushed harder on her clit.

"Is there a reason you're being disobedient?"

"I..." Her whole body shook with the effort to control her reactions.

When she managed to obey, he pulled away from her. She let out a deep, shuddering breath. Whether it was from frustration or relief, he wasn't sure.

He dampened his fingers inside her pussy, then pressed a finger to her anal whorl. "Should I do this, little one?"

In invitation, she swayed.

The throb in his dick became an ache. He wanted to stake his claim on her. "Such a good sub. That's it. Keep your cheeks wide." He pushed past the tightest muscles.

She sighed.

"You like this."

"Yes, Sir."

"Will you like it as much when I shove my cock up here and take you hard?"

Her grip faltered as he pulled out a little before surging in again.

He finger-fucked her ass several times before withdrawing. "How many times a day should I inspect you, Hannah?"

"As many as you'd like, Sir."

A weekend might not be enough. "You may straighten up." His voice was strangled. Did she have any idea how much he desired her?

He helped her up and steadied her while she faced him.

"How does your ass feel?"

"Tingly."

"I'm going to like keeping it full. Something we'll both enjoy. Spread your legs, please. I won't have you trying to relieve your horniness."

Momentarily she closed her eyes, but she nodded.

Mason crossed back to the side of the room to wash his hands and to refocus. He knew of his reputation at the club, as a man who never wanted the same woman twice, always on the prowl for a new experience. The truth was, he enjoyed BDSM scenes, no matter who his partner was. He took his time, learned her nuances, but kept himself at a distance. With Hannah, that was impossible.

He couldn't remember the last time he wanted to fuck a woman senseless. And now, hunger for her consumed him.

Her breaths were soft on the air separating them, and he concentrated on the sound, and the scent of her—vanilla and surrender.

How would she feel in his arms, in his bed?

In frustration, he wadded the paper towel he'd been using and tossed it into the trash can.

Reminding himself to block out everything but the moment, he returned to her. "Now for your breasts."

He cupped them, and they spilled over his palms. "You know I'm going to fuck them, right?"

She moaned, then again louder when he rubbed her nipples.

"Are they sensitive, Hannah?"

"A little. But I like it hard."

"Do you?"

Her lips were parted, and her eyes were pleading.

They were two individuals who needed something only the other could provide. That created understanding. And risk. What happened when their time together ended?

Using his thumbs, he traced her areolas, not touching her nipples.

"Mason…"

"Tell me what you want."

"Squeeze. Pinch."

He gave them the lightest of touches. "Like this?"

"No."

"This, perhaps?" He squeezed until her eyelids drifted shut. She did like it hard. His inner beast liked that. "Should I bring you to your knees?" Between his thumbs and forefingers, he compressed her delicate flesh.

She grabbed his biceps.

"Use your slow word when it's too much." He exerted

even more pressure, and the distinct scent of her reached his nose.

Her eyes closed as she tipped back her head.

"Look at me," he reminded her.

Hannah, wonderful in so many ways, locked her gaze on him.

"That's it." He tugged her nipples up and added a slight twist.

"My God. I want to come."

"Can you? From the nipple stimulation alone?"

"Yes…" Her eyes silently pleaded with him.

"Hannah, Hannah." At that moment, he'd do anything for her. "Tell me what you need."

"I'm so close, Sir. Almost…"

Understanding, he twisted a little more.

She went limp, which tugged more forcefully on her nipples. Screaming out her pleasure, she let go of him. Mason moved his hand to catch her, supporting her weight, then carrying her back to the chair to pull her against his chest. She rested her head on his shoulder, and he stroked back her hair.

"That was hot," he murmured.

"I—I—" She flattened her palm on his chest and pushed away from him. "Wow. I haven't come that hard in years."

"We may need to get you a pair of nipple clamps so I can eat you out while you climax."

She searched his gaze.

"You're wondering if I'm serious. I am." Winding a lock of her hair around his hand, he answered her unasked question. "I most certainly am."

"I'm going to fantasize about that. You know that, Sir?"

Hopefully for months, even after their weekend ended. That idea filled him with a stunning amount of pride. "So now that you've had an orgasm, it's time to get on with your first spanking. Eight, was it?"

"Yes, Sir. Eight."

The climax seemed to have liberated her, settled her into their roles. She sat a little straighter, angled her chin with more confidence. Every moment with her was getting better. "What shall we begin the weekend with?"

She hesitated. "Whatever you prefer, Mason."

His hand itched to connect with her buttocks. Yet his inner Dom needed to flex his muscles. A flogger wouldn't suit his needs. He wanted to mark her. "Dragon's tail."

"Mmm. Where would you like me, Sir?"

"Hands flat on the seat of the chair. Your legs apart. No protecting your pretty little pussy from me."

He expected her to hesitate. Instead she gently slid from his lap.

From the moment he'd first seen her, he'd been determined to have her. Now? Now he knew this taste would not be enough.

CHAPTER 4

Hannah settled into the position, placing her palms flat on the seat of the chair.

Already, this experience had been amazing, overwhelming her in the best possible way.

Witnessing the scene with the Dom and his sub in the medical exam room had stolen her breath. Mason had been attuned to her reactions, so much so that once they were alone, he put his own personal spin on it.

As he traced her eyebrow with incredible gentleness, she was aware that his skin was work roughened…at odds with his handsome tuxedo and businesslike demeanor. He owned a construction firm, but until a few minutes ago, she hadn't realized he did some of the work himself. Calluses like that didn't come from looking at blueprints and spending his days talking to architects.

Putting her name forward for the slave auction was the bravest thing she'd done since leaving Liam. Plenty of times, she'd picked up the phone to call Fiona to insist she couldn't go through with it.

Now, waiting for her Dom's lash, Hannah couldn't believe she'd stayed away from the lifestyle for so long.

She'd allowed her terrible experiences with her ex to change her life, and now she was reclaiming it. And she couldn't be happier.

Ever since he placed the winning bid, Mason handled her skillfully, from coming backstage to taking her someplace to talk. He was the perfect Dom for her reintroduction to BDSM. And that wasn't even factoring in the exquisite orgasm she just had. It was powerful, as energizing as it was relaxing. If she had another dozen or so, she might be able to sleep the entire night.

"The first few won't count."

His words, delivered in an uncompromising tone, jolted her from her musings. "Sir?"

"Were you not listening to me, Hannah?"

"I'm sorry, Sir." She turned her head a little so that she could look at him. Her mouth dried at the sight of the red-handled dragon's tail dangling from his right hand. "I was…"

He waited.

"Thinking how wonderful you are."

"Oh Hannah. That wasn't said to get me to go easy on you."

It was sincere, and she appreciated that he realized it.

"No, Sir. I didn't know who would bid on me." *If anyone.* For weeks, if not months, she'd believed Liam's taunts, that she wasn't sexy enough, curvy enough, submissive enough. When Jax asked for seven thousand dollars, and silence had echoed through the club, shame had washed through her. Liam's words echoed over and over. *Not enough.* But in seconds, Mason had slayed her demons. "I'm glad you did."

He crouched beside her. As he had earlier, he took hold of her chin. He kissed her, in the most tender way possible, then replied. "I'm glad I did, too."

As he released her, she closed her eyes.

"Please give me your full attention."

She blinked him into focus.

"You will know when I begin to give you the eight stripes that you deserve. Until then, don't bother counting."

Warm-up spanks. "Yes, Sir."

"You were listening this time."

Mason started above the backs of her knees and worked his way up her legs—inside, outside, beneath her buttocks, on her ass cheeks, changing directions—never letting her know what to expect.

They were sharp little stings, not lasting more than a moment or two, all delivered from different angles, some straight across, others diagonally.

Hannah allowed her head to drop forward, surrendering her body to his satisfying strokes.

Surprising her, she began to get aroused again.

"Stunning." As he murmured approval, he skimmed a knuckle down her spine.

Instinctively she thrust her hips back a little.

"That's it. Are you ready for more?"

"Yes, Sir."

"Eight."

With him, she didn't tense at all. Instead, she waited. Trusted.

The first lick was so shocking that she curled her fingers.

He paused to draw his finger across the leather's path. "That red mark looks pretty on your skin."

Mason was close enough to fill her senses, with his deep, soothing baritone and commanding touch. On her next breath, she inhaled him—springtime, with its relentless promise of renewal. Right now, she clung to that as if it were a promise.

He gave her plenty of time to recover, enough that the

pain vanished entirely. And she found she missed it. "Another, Sir."

"I'll set the pace, little one. I enjoy your responses, the small welt, the way your body moves, and surely, the way you will fatigue from being in that position, which will cause you to struggle to follow my orders. Or perhaps you'll give yourself over to me entirely and cease caring about how you look."

His frighteningly perceptive words made her freeze.

"You're in your head, Hannah. That's completely fine. When I'm doing my job as I should, perhaps when we repeat this later, you'll lose yourself. I'm looking forward to it because it will mean you trust me enough that you'll show me the real you."

Was she hiding?

The suggestion made her shake her head. She was being as real as she knew how.

While she was still turning the idea around, he striped her again, on the fleshy part of her left ass cheek.

She curved her hands into even tighter fists.

His next two were on her upper right thigh, in that tender spot right beneath her buttock.

"Halfway. Take a break if you need it."

A break?

"You know what to expect now. That should make it easier."

She pushed herself upright to look at him. He hung the dragon's tail from the back of the chair, then folded his arms across his broad chest. His bowtie was still in place, and his starched shirt was snowy against his tanned skin.

He continued to regard her, and she shifted beneath his penetrating stare, very much aware of her nudity, her submissiveness.

To escape his scrutiny, Hannah wrapped her arms around herself.

"I like to look."

Liam certainly hadn't.

But she nodded and lowered her arms to her sides

"Much better." He reached for her, to toy with her nipples, not hard enough for her tastes, but a tease that left her needy.

"I like this. Keeping your awareness high. It will keep your attention on me."

"Sir, all my attention is yours already."

"Is it? Is it really? Or are you spending some time in your head?"

She sighed, and it took all her willpower not to hide from him again.

"Maybe, since we only have a short time together, you can tell me about it?"

"You paid an outrageous amount of money for a weekend with me." She gave him a seductive smile, or what she hoped passed as one. "Are you sure you want to *talk* instead of play?"

"The better I know you, the better the scene."

"I'm ready to proceed whenever you are, Sir."

A smile tugged at his lips, and he appeared to struggle to hold it back. "I do believe that was your polite way of telling me to fuck off."

"Please don't make me use the impolite version. Sir." But with his nonjudgmental reaction, he'd chipped away at the wall she'd constructed around her emotions.

He unfolded his arms. "Give me the dragon's tail, Hannah."

Relieved, she blew out a breath. "Yes, Sir." Fortunately, following his order allowed her to look away from his eyes and to shift her focus, both small mercies.

His hand was extended, and she placed the implement in his palm. "Thank you. You may resume your position."

This was why she'd wanted to attend the slave auction. The protocol involved in a scene grounded her with a sense of purpose, and the bites of leather transformed into pleasure.

Once again, she bent to flatten her hands on the chair, and she parted her legs, ready for whatever he had in mind.

He moved behind her, then came in close enough that his trousers touched her skin. He made small circles on her back and made his way down to her buttocks. "Not a single mark remains."

Hannah hoped that wouldn't be the case after the weekend. She wanted something to remember him by.

He held each of her legs, and she imagined he was checking them for marks as well.

"The warm-up was effective."

Instead of spanking her this time, he forcefully rubbed her thighs and buttocks. He moved her around, and she fought to stay in position. She wasn't aware of him taking his hands off her or moving away, and his first strike seared, catching her off guard.

Instead of crying out, she sighed. It came from somewhere deep, a place she'd buried, one that was hungry.

It hurt.

It was perfect.

Hannah rolled her shoulders and settled in once again. Another hundred of those wouldn't be enough.

He was measured as he was miserly, and he hung the flogger from the chair after he'd delivered the remaining stripes.

Like a proper Dom, he massaged the places the dragon's tail had landed.

She sighed again, this time from disappointment that it was already over.

He helped her to stand, and he cupped her shoulders. "How was it?"

"Thank you. Those last four were wonderful."

"And?"

She searched his eyes. Was he asking for reassurance that he was a good Dom? Wondering if she was mentally and physically all right? Or was he seeking honesty? That was where she'd learned to be careful. Liam never wanted feedback on a scene. "I'm doing fine. Thank you."

"Good." He sat. "Get dressed, please."

His command confused her.

"Feel free to take your time."

Hannah drew her eyebrows together. "Are we finished?" He'd secured a private room and bought over five hundred dollars' worth of toys—not to mention condoms—just for them to leave?

"For the evening? No. I'd like to take you home, after we talk."

He was so confoundingly unlike any other Dom she'd known.

But he was man enough to enjoy watching her work the bikini bottoms up her legs, then settle the string into place between her ass cheeks.

The top was a little more of a challenge. She thought he might offer to help, but he didn't. Instead, he was fixated on her hardened nipples.

She scooped up the filmy sarong and knotted it at the shoulder, not as nicely as Fiona had earlier. Finally, she slipped her feet back into the high heels. Even in those, she hadn't reached his chin earlier.

"And now, you may see to my needs." He extended an

arm, and she rolled down the sleeves, aware of his honed strength.

After finishing, she moved on to the next one before crossing the room to pick up his cufflinks.

They were heavy, and one of them winked in the light. "Are the owl's eyes emeralds?"

"Yes."

"And real gold?" She closed her hand around the precious metal.

Hannah looked at him anew. When she'd had her fantasy about him earlier in the evening, she hadn't suspected that he was the kind of man who had tens of thousands of dollars to spend on a weekend. The cufflinks warming in her hand had to have cost a small fortune.

Under his watchful gaze, she returned to him.

"Judging?"

"No." But was she? She didn't hang out in circles with the ultrarich or even the sort-of rich. Her parents had divorced when she was young. Though they both worked hard, money was always tight. Christmas gifts had often been secondhand, and back-to-school outfits had been purchased at the thrift shop. After graduation, Hannah had attended a junior college while she worked to save money, and studied hard to transfer to a bigger four-year institution. "I'm just curious." In her job as a corporate travel associate, she booked trips all over the world for the company's leaders. She dealt with their assistants and never with the executives themselves.

She was familiar with some of the planet's most luxurious resorts because she was involved in planning the board of director's annual retreat. Because they could write off the expense, it was generally held in some exotic location, places that were out of reach for her.

Driving from Austin to New Orleans was her version of a vacation.

Mason cleared his throat, and she shook her head to clear it. "Sorry, Sir." Her heels tapped on the wood floor as she walked toward him. In front of him, she stood between his spread thighs to thread the pricey pieces of metal through the cuffs on his shirt.

"Very nice." He placed his hands on her hips and moved her back a couple of steps so he could stand. "My jacket?"

"Of course." She held it for him while he slipped it on. Automatically, she brushed the shoulders, then walked around him to smooth the lapels.

Doing personal tasks for a Dom was new for her as well. It was intimate, and she enjoyed it more than she imagined she might.

After he packed the dragon's tail and stowed her collar in one of the bag's compartments, Mason used a wipe to sanitize the chair and the tabletop.

Once he faced her, nerves fluttered anew. She'd had a taste of his dominance, and it had ignited a craving. The floggers were inside his bag, and she wanted to feel both of them on her skin. And then there was the box of condoms.

Suddenly she realized her palms were still on his jacket. Though he studied her, he said nothing as she pulled away.

"Shall we?"

This time, he placed his hand in the middle of her back as they exited, then descended the stairs to find a snuggle couch.

"This really isn't necessary, Sir," she said when he sat beside her on the overstuffed velvet cushions.

"I thought we should talk for a minute."

And she wanted to continue to play. Eight strokes, no matter how well delivered, could hardly be counted as a scene.

"You're okay?"

She nodded.

"Nothing too much for you?"

"Just your relentless questions." Instantly she regretted her answer. "I apologize. That was too honest."

He grinned while she twisted her fingers together. Then she tried, in her own awkward way, to make amends.

"But the lashes were wonderful."

"And harder would have been fine?" he surmised. "Along with a higher number of strokes?"

"Yes, Sir."

"Good." He nodded. "Good to know."

As if they were longtime lovers, he brushed her hair aside and made absent circles on her nape.

Until she closed her eyes, she didn't realize she'd been holding on to some tension.

"I'm glad you're letting your guard down." He continued his light massage as he spoke. "I'd like for you to come back to my house, but I will understand if that makes you uncomfortable. I imagine you're in a hotel? Or perhaps staying with friends?"

"With Fiona. She was in the auction also."

"If it's better for you, we can just plan to meet tomorrow morning and take it from there."

She sat up so she could face him. Being accommodating hadn't helped with Liam. Instead, it had left her unsatisfied. This time, with a new Dom, she had a chance to start over and do things differently. And that included speaking up. "I'd like to go home with you, Sir."

"Do you have everything you need to spend the night?"

"I have a bag, yes. Toiletries, a change of clothes."

"Excellent." He didn't stop his tender motions. "That was the answer I was hoping for."

~

"This is where you live?" With shock and not a little amount of awe, she looked up at the stunning two-story white house with its wrought-iron double porches.

"Long story."

"I'm looking forward to all the details."

He used a remote control to open the gate, and when he parked, she reached for the door handle.

"Wait for me. Please."

Hannah dropped her hand into her lap. "Of course, Sir." No one had ever helped her from a car before, and waiting for him to grab his bag and round the hood made her a little uncomfortable.

He opened her door and offered his hand. The moment she slid her palm against his, everything was right with the world again. He wasn't like any other man, but there was a natural order to their relationship that she liked. "Thank you."

When she was away from the vehicle, he flicked the door closed.

The heavy spring air wrapped around her like a cloying blanket, but even that didn't distract from her fascination with his house. "Your home is stunning."

"Three years ago, it wasn't."

Of course. He was in construction.

He invited her through the courtyard.

"This is a fabulous space." She looked around. There were no tables or chairs, yet there was plenty of room for one. "A lot of potential."

"Are you remodeling it in your head?"

"No." She followed him up the couple of stairs leading to the back door. "Well, maybe thinking about a gazebo. And a table with chairs."

"You *are* remodeling."

They entered a mudroom where he hung his bag. "You're

welcome to leave your belongings here. Or there's a table in the foyer, if you prefer."

"Thanks. I'll put them closer to where I'll need them."

She followed him into a kitchen that was a chef's dream, and hers too. The countertops appeared to be quartz, and there was a gigantic island. She trailed her fingers over the edge. "I love this waterfall style."

"One of the features I decided on by myself. The gray cabinets, the backsplash, that's all the designer."

"She did a nice job." Hannah glanced at the pot filler and the six-burner stove. "Do you cook?"

"No."

So all this was lost on him.

"It's great for entertaining."

"Do you do a lot of that?"

"I've hosted a couple of events here, including Getting Hammered."

She frowned. "What's that?"

"It's a preservation fundraising event. Every month, we meet at a house that's being restored. We have beer and—"

"I get it." She grinned. "Hammers and hammered. Play on words."

"You're fast." He tipped a mock hat in her direction. "Would you like to see the house so you can be comfortable?"

"Every inch."

"There's a lot of them."

Did she ever have to leave?

"Let's start at the front door, so you can appreciate the whole thing."

The attention to detail was jaw-dropping, from ceiling medallions to polished wood floors.

A gorgeous fireplace dominated the foyer.

"It's original, but no longer operational, unfortunately. At one time it provided heat for the entire house."

"The mantelpiece is breathtaking."

"The home was built for the Manvilles as a wedding gift from the groom's father. They enjoyed traveling around the world, and Mrs. Manville had it sent over from Italy when she was on vacation."

Hannah set her purse on the table he'd indicated, and he placed his bag on the floor before leading her into the ballroom. "The windows open up all the way so you can walk outside. When the house was first built, a carriage could draw up to the house for events. The occupants would alight onto the porch, then walk straight into the home, bypassing the door."

"Ingenious."

"There are blinds, here." He unfolded them from inside the wall.

"I've never seen anything like it."

"It was quite the find. Hidden behind some paint."

"Paint?"

"Purple. From the 1970s, we guessed. By then, the house had been subdivided into two apartments. It's the longest demo I've ever been involved with."

They walked through to the dining room. She guessed the oversize table seated twenty, but right now, most of it was covered with paper—blueprints, design magazines, sketches, notes, real estate listings. "Your office?"

"It's not supposed to be. But once I grab my coffee in the morning, I often gravitate to this room before heading to work. It's..."

She waited. He hadn't hesitated before now.

"A sense of family. Connection."

An interesting thing for the infamous One Night Dom to say.

"Let's go this way." He took her back to the foyer, then into what she guessed was a living room, since it had a large-screen television and comfortable-looking couch. While the picture rail and crown molding appeared to be original, the furnishings were modern and inviting. Dozens of books were artfully displayed on shelves, and she could imagine curling up with a cup of tea and spending the day lost between the covers.

"This," he said, walking through the opening that could be blocked off with pocket doors, "is supposed to be my study."

At one end of the room was a brown leather couch. Despite having end tables adorned with beautiful Tiffany-style lamps, and a colorful afghan draped across one of the arms, the piece of furniture was too big to be inviting.

An imposing rolltop desk was the room's focal point, and it had an old-fashioned rolling wood chair tucked beneath it. The blinds were closed, and the lightbulbs weren't bright enough for the large space. Plants might help. Different colors, anything to break the masculine monochrome. "I see why you don't use it."

"Oh?" He folded his arms across his chest.

"I don't mean to be offensive."

"Not at all."

"It's more sterile than the rest of the rooms. Darker. Somber." A little sad. Lonely, even.

For a moment, Hannah thought he might say something, but he didn't.

"But suddenly I'm imagining you splayed wide, your back arched, tied to the desk."

She blinked as her breathing slowed. After they'd left the private room at the Quarter, she'd claimed her purse and large tote bag from the cloakroom. Then she'd changed into her street clothes—a little black dress, pearls she'd bought herself with her first ever bonus, and heels.

When she emerged from the small locker room, he'd given her an appreciative glance before escorting her down the stairs and out of the club. Because her heels would make it difficult for her to walk to his car, he'd hired a bicycle rickshaw to shuttle them the few blocks.

During the ride through the crowded streets of the French Quarter, then the drive to the Lower Garden District, Mason had kept the conversation casual, with no hint of what they'd shared or what the weekend held. So his words now caught her completely off guard.

"It would be the perfect way to flog you."

"A desk as bondage equipment?"

"Finally the room has merits."

She hesitated. This was one of the most unnerving parts about playing with someone new…the uncertainty. Did he mean it? Or was it a merely a tease, part of engaging her mind as well as her body. "I'm not sure whether or not you're serious."

"I assure you, I am." His face was set in hard lines, and his eyes were unreadable. "What do you say, Hannah? Are you going to turn yourself over to me?"

As if that were in doubt.

Devilishly, he smiled.

"Since we both know your answer, take off your dress."

CHAPTER 5

Hannah had wanted to continue their encounter, but stripping in his study and being tied up to his desk was so far out of her expectations that the world spun a little faster.

"Shall we start with your front or your back?"

A wicked thrill turned her tummy. "Whatever you say, Sir." She reached behind her for the zipper's hasp but fumbled with it.

"May I?"

"Please." She turned her back to him, and he brushed her hair aside. He placed a small kiss on the side of her neck before finishing the task.

She was tempted to lean into him, but he'd given her an order.

Obediently, she lifted the dress up and off.

Mason took it from her and draped it over the chair.

"And the lingerie. Which is beautiful, by the way."

Matching and new, black satin and lace, and so far above her budget that she'd justified it as a once-in-a-lifetime splurge. She'd hoped someone would bid on her, and if so, she'd hoped he was a Dom who appreciated beautiful undergarments.

Hannah worked her panties down her legs, then unfastened her bra and rolled her shoulders forward so the straps fell.

He placed each piece with her dress. "Would you like to wear the pearls or remove them?"

She twirled one of the white beads. "Do you have a preference?"

He perused her. "Looking at you in your heels and pearls is the stuff of fantasies. If I was having you pose for pictures, that's what I would have you wear. But I don't want them to get damaged or broken."

"I agree."

"I'll put them back when I'm done with you. Lift your hair so I can help you."

She thought he might fumble since his fingers were so big and roughened, but he effortlessly unfastened the latch.

He placed the necklace on top of her dress, in a long, snaking angle that revealed an artistic flair. Another facet of him that she hadn't expected.

Mason pushed the chair toward a corner, out of the way. "Wait for me here. I'll be gone less than five minutes."

"Yes, Sir."

At the doorway, he paused to brace a hand on the frame. He turned back to face her. "Will you be okay if I leave you alone? That was on your limits list..."

He remembered, and he cared. The difference between him and Liam had never been starker than at this moment. "I'm okay."

Concern, and a little doubt, furrowed his eyebrows, so she offered a further explanation, revealing parts of herself that she'd kept hidden until now. "That's more about humiliation." Being put on show. Or worse, abandoned. "You're not leaving me to"—*shame*—"ignore me, Sir."

"You're welcome to come with me."

Her clothes were in the room, and her purse was in the kitchen. She wasn't tied up. At any point, she could dress and leave at any time she wanted, and that was all the security she needed. "Thank you. I really am fine."

"If you change your mind, call for me. Or come and find me."

Then he left. Suddenly the room chilled by several degrees—either that or her imagination was in fine form.

Nerves.

It had to be nerves.

At home, she never went nude. She slept in shorts and tank top, and even after a bath, she slipped into a robe, so it was strange, being alone, naked in his study.

The air conditioner kicked on, making her nipples hard again and chilling her body. Restless, she walked around the room, and her heels were the only sound in the silent house.

For a moment, she stopped to listen deeper, trying to discern where Mason was and what he was doing. No doubt he'd gone to retrieve his bag with the toys he'd paid an exorbitant sum for. But that wouldn't take this long.

A faint creak reached her. His footfall on the stairs? He'd mentioned tying her up. Was he fetching rope?

Her nerves ratcheted up again.

Several pictures hung from the far wall—drawings of some kind. Homes in the area? She moved in for a closer view. At least one of them appeared to be of his house. And another she recognized from a tour she'd taken. They were all signed in the same way, and she realized they were renderings, all from the same architect. Someone prominent, no doubt.

She studied each picture several times, trying to keep her

thoughts from spiraling out of control, wondering what was going to happen when he returned.

Another creak drifted on the air.

Then he was back, still wearing his dress slacks and shirt, but he'd taken off his jacket, the cummerbund, and the bowtie. He'd removed a couple of the pearl studs, and he'd rolled up his shirtsleeves.

He held a black leather monogrammed bag, and he carried it to a side table. "Come here, Hannah."

His voice was deep with uncompromising command, and she took smaller than usual steps as she went to him.

"Go ahead. Have a look."

She loosened the latch and lifted it. The small flogger was there, along with skeins of rope, safety scissors, two pairs of nipple clamps, a bottle of lubricant, a package of hand sanitizing wipes, and a medium-size silicone butt plug.

Under his watchful gaze, she took out each item and placed them next to each other.

"Choose which nipple clamps you wish to wear."

The tweezers were thick and sturdy, but she picked the clovers. She tested the grip on her pinky finger, then immediately removed them. "These, Sir," she said, selecting the less vicious ones.

"Now let me see you put them on."

Though she often wore them when she masturbated, it took her a couple of attempts since he was right there, smelling of spice and intent, planning to flog her.

"They look lovely."

She swayed a little to test them. They were affixed well enough that they wouldn't slip off, but they weren't so tight that they ached.

"Are you aroused?"

"The clamps alone aren't doing it, to be honest, Sir."

"Perhaps a little ass play may help?"

Hannah already knew his tone well enough to know that wasn't a suggestion.

"Go ahead and put lube on the plug." He leaned his shoulders against the wall. "You'll want to put on plenty so it goes in easier."

After squirting a generous dollop of the viscous fluid into her palm, she coated the entire length of the shaft. While it was thicker at the base than anything she owned, it wasn't outrageously big.

"Make sure you work it back and forth."

As if I'm lubing your cock? For a moment, lost, she hesitated.

"Now me." He extended his hand.

She placed the silicone toy upright on the table, then coated his first two fingers.

"You think that's enough? It's your ass in question."

To be sure, and because he obviously liked it, she did it one more time before cleaning her hands on one of the wipes.

"I'd like you to bend your knees a little and spread your ass for me, and don't even think of a halfhearted attempt like you tried to get away with at the club."

She opened her mouth to protest. Then she remembered his masterful handling of her and the way he'd parted her cheeks farther than she imagined possible.

Without any further hesitation, she followed his instructions. The clamps swayed, exerting a minute amount of pressure. It wasn't enough to arouse her, just snare her attention.

"Good."

His approval meant the world to her. He slipped a finger into her rear channel, somewhat faster than he had earlier this evening. Because of the lube and because they'd done this once, it wasn't a struggle at all, and she was ready for him. "Sir…"

When he pushed forward again, it was with two fingers.

She was so full that she sighed. Even though she said nothing, clearly he knew what she wanted, and he thrust his fingers in and out of her several times. Then he finger-fucked her relentlessly until she whimpered, on the verge of an orgasm.

"If I touch your clit, you'll come, won't you?"

Suddenly the thought was at the forefront of her mind. "Yes."

"Then I'll be sure not to do that."

Her hands slipped, but before she uttered a protest, she pulled her ass cheeks apart for him again.

Mason drove back inside her, deep, all the way to his knuckles, filling her completely. He was fast, more powerful than before, rocking her forward onto her toes and tugging uncomfortably on her clamps.

After pulling out and plunging back in, he scissored his fingers apart, making her gasp. "Oh, Sir!"

"I like filling you, Hannah."

"Yes, yes!"

And then…he pulled out and moved away from her. With her hands braced on her knees, she tried to catch her breath.

Since he hadn't given her permission to move, she stayed where she was, wide open, needy, the clamps swinging back and forth.

His shoes were loud over the rushing in her head, and she guessed he was at the table, wiping his hands.

"I'm going to enjoy this at least as much as you do," he said as he returned.

He pressed the tip of the plug to her, then slid an arm beneath her tummy to hold her in place as he inserted the large piece of silicone.

When he reached the fattest part, she whimpered. She

was sure Mason had fully prepared her for it, and when she'd coated the thing, it hadn't seemed as big as it did now.

He drew the shaft back an inch or so, giving her a chance to relax for a moment before trying again.

"That's... It's a lot, Sir."

"Before this weekend is out, I intend to fuck your ass with my cock. I suggest you take every opportunity to get used to it."

Her head swam. He was the perfect combination of forceful and kind, the swoon-worthy kind of Dom she dreamed of.

"Ask for it."

He was demanding the impossible.

"But..."

"I'm waiting."

Nothing could be worse than him just holding it there. She fidgeted, trying to get some relief.

"We've got all night." His tone was patient, and the only way he'd relent was if she used a safe word. And things weren't that bad.

Fine. He won. "I'd like it inside me."

"You've stalled so long I'd like to hear a little more enthusiasm."

She wrinkled her nose. Her legs were fatiguing, and the pressure on her nipples was becoming intolerable. When she was sexually aroused, wearing clamps heightened her pleasure. Now the ache was an unwelcome distraction. "Will you put the plug all the way in me, Sir?"

"Anything for you, Hannah." He held her tighter and then sank the plug in all the way.

She yelped as the widest part pushed past her sphincter, and then...blessed relief. The stem was a fraction of the diameter, and her body was able to relax.

"I can't tell you how nice that looks all snuggled up in

there." He lowered his arm but took a second to touch her shoulder reassuringly before leaving her.

He returned to wipe off the excess lube before letting her know it was okay to stand up.

"Thank you, Sir." As she turned toward him, the floor seemed to move beneath her. Mason was there for her, reaching out with a steadying hand. "I'm good. Just stood up too fast."

As if wanting to be sure for himself, he held on to her for a few seconds before he spoke again. "How does that feel? Is the plug big enough for you?"

She wasn't sure she understood his question. It was larger than she was accustomed to.

"I want to be sure you're aware of its presence. There's a larger one I can fetch, if you'd prefer?"

"No!"

His grin was sexy and triumphant.

"I can definitely feel it."

"Perhaps I should inspect you."

Lord save her. He couldn't know how his words undid her. She dreaded that as much as she thirsted for it.

"That wasn't a random musing."

Heat poured through her at his implacable tone. Understanding his unspoken command, she instantly spread her legs, making the toy shift. She placed her hands behind her neck. The combination of his attention and the way the clamps tugged was overwhelming.

"I may require you to be in that position all the time, with your entire body available to me."

Yes.

He cupped the base of her skull in his palm so she couldn't escape, not that she would ever try. "How are the clamps? Tight enough?" Rather than waiting for a response, he tugged on the chain, making her moan. "The clovers would be better if we were having a long, drawn-out scene, wouldn't they?" He exerted more force, not a lot, just enough. "They'd stay on, tightening even, if I yanked."

His words were enough to make her thoughts collide.

He dropped the chain, and the slight downward force shot pleasure through it. It wasn't from the clamps, she realized with shocking clarity, but from his proximity.

Mason took a breath and studied her nipples. "A little swollen already. The compression marks will be sexy. I can't wait to see them."

Which no doubt meant he wouldn't be loosening the slide anytime soon.

Instead of moving on, he pinched one of her nipples. The pain was sensational. He backed off a little to roll it gently, soothing the hurt he'd inflicted. Just as she closed her eyes, he squeezed again, dragging her back to full consciousness.

"That's better," he said when her attention was focused on him.

A few seconds later, he loosened his grip and traced his way down her rib cage. The nipple he hadn't touched throbbed with demand.

He skimmed across her pubic area, then eased a finger between her pussy lips. "It seems you like what we're doing."

"What you're doing."

"No mistake, Hannah. This is *us.* Not me. If you weren't into it, it wouldn't matter how I handled you—roughly or with care. Your mind has to be in the right place for this to be so arousing."

In that case, he was definitely right.

He made the tiniest of circles on her clit. If he continued that, she would come in seconds. Silently asking for that, she jutted her hips forward. Inside her, the toy moved, ratcheting up her desire.

"I want to know how full the plug makes you."

Again, she knew he wasn't asking for her permission but rather telling her what he was going to do, which increased the power of his mindfuck.

He slid two fingers inside her. From that position, he could reach her G-spot. But, horrible torment that he was, he didn't. Instead, imprisoning her gaze as surely as he did her head, he began to insert a third finger.

There was no way she could do this. She was too full of the plug to take any more of him.

"You're wet enough." His voice soothed, as if he read her fears. "You've got a slow word and a safe word. If it hurts, be sure to tell me to stop. But if it's just your brain trying to convince you that you can't, that you shouldn't, that it's impossible, then try to work through it. I've got you." His words were hypnotic. She was half-aware of him relentlessly persisting, not changing a single thing. "Remember the submissive at the club? What did her top do to her?"

"Placed her feet in the stirrups, Sir." He was right that her pussy was slick for him. He was stretching her, and it was a little uncomfortable, mostly because she was standing, but it didn't hurt in the least.

"What was he doing?"

"Examining her."

"Yes. He wasn't allowing her any secrets, was he? He wanted to see every part of her."

Technically, the woman had on a T-back thong, but it had covered so little that it was all but useless. Watching sub and Dom play together had been hot. And the knowledge that Mason remembered what aroused her gave her a cupful of courage.

He spread his fingers then, and she was full of him. Keeping his gaze on her, he simulated having sex, working back and forth, a little deeper each time, demanding more from her and her body.

Putting her hands on him for reassurance, she bent her knees a little more.

Dark spikes of approval appeared in his green eyes. That her actions pleased him made her soar. She could survive for days from that.

He placed his thumb on her clit and compressed the swollen flesh.

"God almighty." She grasped him tighter.

"Can you come?"

"Sir… I'm not…" Not sure. There was so much pressure, too many sensations, and she wasn't sure her body was capable of more.

"If you can, you may."

She closed her eyes in surrender.

"That's it, Hannah. Give yourself over to me. I'll keep you safe."

He circled her clit as he relentlessly filled her pussy. Could he feel the plug sliding around?

Impossibly, he silently asked for more, stretching her. Harsher… All his fingers? His knuckles? No. He couldn't be doing what she imagined. Could he? There was no way she was capable of that.

Then he kissed her, with infinite tenderness. That was too much. The combination of his taste, his demands, the way he handled her, the pain, the torment, the way her clit throbbed.

He rubbed her clit, and she had to turn her head to escape him so she could scream out her orgasm.

There was a wrinkle in the time-space continuum, and when she returned from the stratosphere, he was murmuring her name. She liked the sound of it so well that she didn't respond for a moment.

"You're more than I could have imagined."

Mason was still cradling her head, supporting her body, but she had dropped her hands. He brushed across her clit once again, then withdrew from her pussy. Every part of her ached, but she wasn't distressed in the least. "We didn't just do what I thought we did. Did we?" She frowned, trying to piece together exactly what had happened, but there were too many sensations to sort through. "Tell me that didn't just happen."

"Well, if you think you were amazing, that happened." He grinned. "And if you came when I played with your clit, that happened. Inspecting you? That also happened."

"But… I mean. I can't… I haven't." She shook her head. "Never."

"Yeah. You can. You have."

"In that case, I might be a little freaked out."

He picked her up and carried her to the couch. She expected him to sit next to her. Instead, he scooped her into his lap.

His cock was hard, yet he said nothing about it, seemingly focused exclusively on her.

"Let's get the nipple clamps off. At least for the time being."

He pinched the tweezer tip between a finger and thumb as he lowered the slide mechanism. Then very slowly, he eased it off so that blood flow didn't return in a rush. "How's that?"

"That's good."

Gently, he continued to massage her.

When he released her, he studied the small indention left behind. "That's really hot."

She was still in a daze as he removed the other one.

"Are you warm enough?" He dropped the clamps onto the side table, then wrapped his arms around her.

"I am now." Hannah was glad for the respite from the

scene. At the club, he hadn't pushed her far enough, and now she was satiated.

He was a fabulous Dominant. Over the years, she'd played with a few men, but none had been this masterful, demanding, and at the same time, approving.

From somewhere in the house, a clock chimed. "Midnight?"

"The witching hour. Ready to go upstairs? Or would you like to continue?"

"Really?" She'd fully expected him to ask for sex after that. No other man had just satisfied her like that, then offered to go on.

"Really." The word was rich with promise as well as warning. Purposefully, he glanced at the rolltop desk.

Suddenly, she had to know. Their time together ended Sunday night, and she returned to Austin midmorning on Monday. This might be a dream, and if it was, Hannah wanted to revel in all the details. "In that case, yes. I'd like to continue."

His eyes brightened. When she'd first studied him, they'd appeared dark, like jade. Now they were more complex, with specks of gold dust.

"I have two choices for you, Hannah."

She shuddered at the purposeful gleam in his eyes.

"Do you want to start with your face forward so that I flog your backside first?" He released her hand. "Or shall we begin with your front so that I can wrap the strands around your breasts, maybe catching your nipples?"

CHAPTER 6

Mason had never been more enchanted by a submissive. When his father was dying, Deborah's selfishness had left Mason wary of relationships, and now Hannah's sweet innocence filled voids he didn't realize he had. He was known as a Dom who took care of the women he spent time with, but this went beyond that. As he'd driven Hannah to his home, his thoughts had been consumed with ways to satisfy her and ensure their weekend was one she'd always remember.

Her unusual-colored eyes were so expressive that she couldn't hide her thoughts from him. Shock. Anticipation. Impatience. Guardedness. Even a soft glow of happiness.

The range of emotions pleased him. Although she didn't know what to expect, she trusted him to set the pace. That she'd done something that stunned her made him proud. Never had he been more aware of his power as a Dom. He savored it. Treasured it. "I suppose there's a third option. You can allow me to make the decision."

"Uhm… Facedown. If it's okay with you, Sir."

"It is, indeed." He jostled her from his lap. "Please go to the table and bring me some rope."

As she crossed the room, her hips swayed a little more than normal, maybe because of the plug. Which was incentive to use a bigger one.

Tapping his fingers on his knee, he remained where he was and waited for her to bring him the hemp. He'd selected red because it would be a sensational contrast to her pale skin. He wasn't wrong.

After he finished securing her ankles to the front legs of the desk, he stepped back, happy with his choice.

He walked around to the far side and asked her to extend her arms as far as was comfortable. Two minutes later, her body was beautifully arched, conforming to the curve of the rolltop. "If I can keep you like this, I will be inspired to use my study more."

She tested her bonds. They had enough give that she could move a little, but not escape. He looked forward to watching her writhe. "Are you comfortable?"

"It's not exactly a spa experience, Mason."

He laughed. "Allow me to rephrase. Are any of your muscles or joints suffering from undue stress?" Some was normal. He intended for her legs to be spread wide, making her body available to him.

"No, Sir."

"And your circulation is okay?"

"Yes."

Even though she said so, he double-checked his knots, making certain he could place a finger between her and the rope. "And the plug is still settled nicely in your bottom?"

She whispered something that might have been, "Oh God."

"I'm afraid I didn't hear you."

"It's fine, Sir." She tried to lift her head, but her movements were too restricted. "Thank you."

"That's what I thought you said." After collecting the flogger, he returned to dance the strands over her body. "This won't be about counting, so don't bother, unless it's something that gives you peace. I'll keep on until I decide you've had enough." There was no way he'd come anywhere close to her needing a safe word. He intended for this to be arousing, not punishing. "No part of your body will be off-limits to me."

Obviously knowing what he meant, she tightened her buttocks and pulled against her bindings, trying to bring her legs together. "That won't save you, darling Hannah." He slapped her ass hard with his hand.

She yelped, then relaxed her body.

"Much better." He stepped back, then adjusted his stance and distance so he could warm up her rear.

With a figure-eight motion, he covered her ass cheeks until they were a delicate pink.

She drew in a breath, then expelled it, which allowed the wood beneath her to support her torso. "That's it."

He moved up to flog her back with the suede, and after a few minutes, he wrapped the falls around her ribs, then the sides of her breasts. "Are your nipples getting hard again?" Not giving her time to answer, he went on. "Maybe you should rub them against the desk, just to be certain." Since the rolltop portion was made up from dozens of slats, there would be plenty of friction.

He put extra force in the next forty or so strokes, ensuring she'd move around.

"Mason! That's—"

"I could clamp your nipples again, if you prefer?"

"No, Sir!" She pressed herself even farther into the desk, and he slid a finger into her heated pussy.

"I might start to think that you like this, Hannah."

"I do!"

So did he. "I like watching you. Keep it up, please."

While she writhed, he changed his angle so he could flog her upper thighs, close, so very close to her waxed pussy.

Her breaths came in frantic bursts, and he knew it took some effort for her not to surrender to her instinctive urge to protect her most private parts.

To keep her guessing, he returned to her ass cheeks. They glowed from his attention. Once again, he realized that selecting the red rope had been the right choice. It was now the same color as her skin, and the hemp would forever remind him of this evening.

Her chest no longer rose and fell so desperately, so he took that moment to land a stroke between her thighs, wrapping upward, between her delicate folds.

She screamed his name.

"Another? Ten? Twenty."

"Yes, yes!" With greater fervor, she ground her breasts into the antique piece as he flogged her pussy with the most delicate licks.

Instead of satisfying her again, he turned away and tossed the flogger on the chair. Her reactions, the musky, feminine scent of her submission, enveloped him. He needed to be inside her, claim her as his own.

Her chest heaved, and he studied her, each rapidly fading mark, and the few pink spots on the sides of her breasts. Through his trousers, he stroked his erect dick. A weekend wasn't nearly long enough for him to drink his fill of her.

Ignoring his cock's incessant demand, he strode to her and unfastened her wrists, checking that they weren't too red. Then he knelt next to her to release her ankles. Being this close to her, smelling her heat, spiked his arousal.

He had tremendous self-control, but at this moment, all his resolve was being tested.

She remained where she was, her beautiful body limp.

"How are you doing?" He stroked her heated back, the warmth in contrast to the coolness of the room.

"Sir, you are just amazing."

"I think the same of you, Miss Hannah." He helped her up, and she turned herself toward him. Trusting.

He led her to the couch and covered her with the throw. She snuggled into him, and he lost track of the amount of time he held her.

When the clock chimed a single time, she lifted her head. "One o'clock?"

"Twelve thirty, I'm guessing." He doubted their scene had lasted an hour, but it was possible. When he was with her, the minutes ticked by too fast. "Tired?"

"Somewhere beyond that, I think."

He'd given her a lot. "Let's go to bed."

Since she didn't seem capable of moving, he placed his hands on her hips and assisted her up. "You can be asleep within five minutes. Promise."

"I'll hold you to that." She kept the small blanket around her as they walked into the foyer.

"Shall I bring up your bag?"

"I'd appreciate that."

She moved up the stairs slowly, as if she had leaden feet. He wasn't sure whether to show some sympathy or congratulate himself on a job well done.

"Will you show me the rest of the house tomorrow?"

"Of course. You can explore to your heart's content. It's the door at the end of the hallway." Though he favored restoration over renovation in historic homes, he liked his creature comforts. He'd converted what had originally been a nursery into a good size closet, and he'd converted a bedroom in to a private bathroom.

He flicked on the light switch.

"This is huge," she exclaimed.

The space was masculine, with a large wardrobe and a four-poster king-size bed. His designer had filled the fireplace opening with candles he'd never lit. But he'd adorned the mantel with pictures of his parents, including the last one he had of his father. It had been taken just weeks before his death. Despite his gaunt features, his smile was wide and hopeful, filled with love.

Mason had added the newest photo last week. Though he'd had it for six months, it had been difficult for him to put it with the rest of the collection. The snapshot was one of his mother, with her boyfriend. Time moved on, Mason recognized. But acceptance was more difficult than anticipated. She deserved to be happy. God knew that. But maybe she could have fallen in love another year from now.

Then again, who knew if he would still struggle?

Tired of brooding, he returned his attention to Hannah. "The bathroom is through there." He pointed.

"Thank you." She walked toward it, and he followed her.

When she saw the room, she gasped. "This looks like something out of a magazine."

"I thought you'd like it."

"You must have been smiling downstairs when I told you that the rolltop desk wasn't exactly a spa experience. Because this really is one."

He grinned. It was. Because he'd constructed with resale value in mind, each detail had been inspired by the city's high-end spas. Though he appreciated the steam shower and used it every day during the winter, he'd stopped noticing the mosaic tile floor. On rare occasions, he opened a drawer. But he almost never used the cabinets.

His housekeeper laundered the towels periodically to keep them fresh. How she had the patience to re-roll them each month or so and tie them with some sort of thick purple string and stack them in symmetrical piles of three, he had no idea.

Now he was glad. "There's a basket over there filled with soaps." He pointed to a teakwood bench. "Another has hair stuff, shampoos and whatnot. I was promised it was good stuff that ladies like."

She grinned at how far out of his element he seemed. "I've never seen a clawfoot tub like that."

"Definitely not original to the house," he agreed. "The feet are supposed to be lions' paws. Unless the designer was joking, and I bought it."

"I bet that's what they're supposed to be." She crouched for a better look. "I like them."

He liked that the faucet was on the side and that it had a handheld shower to go with it. "It's made from acrylic, rather than metal. Better insulation, so it's not as cold when you first get in. Supposed to stay warmer for longer too."

"You don't mind if I use it while I'm here?"

He'd like it if she did. Until now, he hadn't shared it with anyone. "Please do. As many times as you'd like. Make yourself at home." The niceties were wasted on him, but Hannah's joy delighted him. "If you'll bend over the sink, I'll remove your plug."

She wrinkled her nose as she straightened up. "Thank you. I can manage that on my own."

"In that case, I'll leave you to it. Feel free to use the towels. Washcloths are in the linen closet. Anything else you need?"

"Actually, I forgot to bring pajamas."

"Naked is fine."

"How did I know you were going to say that, Sir?"

"I'll find you something to wear." As he left, he closed the door behind him.

Mason grabbed her one of his work T-shirts and draped it over the leather bench at the end of the bed.

While she soaked, he went back downstairs to clean up their toys and to make sure the doors were locked. Then he turned off the lights before returning to the master bedroom.

Hannah stood in front of the fireplace, a towel wrapped turban-style around her head.

She was holding a picture of him with his father. "You look a lot like him."

Their heads were tipped toward each other, and they were both holding up hammers. "It was right after I joined him in the business." When life had been simpler, and before the horrible diagnosis that would come a few years later.

"He looks happy."

"It was a dream. Yes. The company was owned by my great-grandfather, and he was hoping I'd carry on the tradition."

"Always in Louisiana?"

"Yes. My great-grandfather's brother moved first. When we emigrated, my family decided on New Orleans. My great-grandfather's brother had been here for a few years and wrote home with stories about the weather. After a particularly harsh winter, he packed up the family and moved."

"You're an only child?"

"My parents never planned it that way, but yes."

"So am I. My parents divorced early. Probably a good thing there weren't more kids. It was a struggle for my mom after my dad left Texas." She put the picture back, in the precise place it had been. "The logo on your T-shirts is the same as the one I'm wearing."

"It looks much nicer on you." He swept his gaze over her. The material covered her to midthigh, but his imagination filled in the missing details.

"Thank you for letting me use that bath." She took the turban from her head and towel-dried her hair. "I don't suppose you can arrange to have it transported to Austin?"

"As much as I'd like to, probably not."

"I'm sure my apartment superintendent wouldn't approve, anyway."

"Well, you're welcome here anytime."

Hannah walked over to her bag and pulled out a brush. She curled up on his bed, cross-legged, and ran the bristles through the damp length.

Voyeuristically he watched her. Her nipples were hard against his T-shirt, and she seemed lost in thought.

He was more comfortable with her than was possible in this short length of time. It was nice having a woman around, and the scent of something sweet on the air. "You used a soap?"

"It's called Sweet Dreams," she said. "Lavender for relaxation, coconut oils for rehydration, colloidal oatmeal to soothe"

"All that from a bar of soap? I thought it was just for cleaning off the grime."

"You know that statement makes you a heathen, right?"

The only thing he was certain of right now was that he was looking forward to waking up next to her in the morning.

And so was his insistent dick.

~

Hannah blinked her world into focus.

For a moment, she was disoriented. Sunlight streamed through the large windows, unhampered by the sheer curtains covering them.

This wasn't her bedroom, with its thick blinds and

small bed.

Some of her muscles were a bit stiff, and her pussy…

Awareness rushed through her, jolting her awake. She was in New Orleans, in the world's most comfortable bed. At Mason's house.

Slowly she turned over to face him.

In sleep, he appeared much less formidable. Younger. Less overwhelming. No doubt that would change quickly.

After their scene at the Quarter, she'd revised her expectations for the weekend. When she signed up, she'd hoped for something really physical to snap her out of her funk. And while she wanted a high-octane experience, Mason had been kind. Solicitous, even. Eight gentle strokes from a competent Dom. Competent and *nice.*

But here, at his house, he'd taken her places she'd never been. It thrilled her and scared her all at the same time.

But worse were the emotions he'd reawakened in her. She'd spent months burying her past, trying to forget Liam and her experiences with him, and yet they'd shaped so much of who she was and the reasons she'd changed. Things she'd been okay with were now on her limits list. While Mason respected her wishes, he was obviously curious about her. His questions were insightful, and that unnerved her. She knew he wouldn't be satisfied for long. But all she had to do was fend him off for the rest of their time together. Then she'd never see him again, and she could keep her memories where they belonged. In the darkest recesses of her mind.

As if aware of her scrutiny, he opened his eyes. The jade hue was brighter this morning, maybe from the sunshine. "Morning." His voice was husky with sleep, and it sent sexual skitters through her.

"Good morning." She pretended a casualness she didn't feel, telling herself this was an ordinary day with an ordinary man. "Can I hope for coffee in my future?"

"You any good at making it? Because I've been told mine is like tar, only thicker. My mom says mine made her spoon disintegrate the last time she was here."

"It sounds dangerous." Hannah seized the opportunity, not just to put a little distance between them, but to use his kitchen. In Austin, hers was galley-type, with hardly any counter space. The dishwasher door couldn't be lowered all the way without bumping in to cupboards on the opposite side of the kitchen.

"If you don't mind bringing me a cup, we can drink it up here on the gallery."

"Gallery?"

"Porch. It's a regional term, perhaps. When a home has double galleries, it means it has both an upper and lower porch."

"I had no idea."

"I'll tell you more about the house, if you want. You might have seen drawings of it in the study. It was featured in a magazine in the mid-1840s."

"I'd love it. I'm completely enchanted, and I want to know all the details." Though she watched a lot of television shows on the home improvement channels, getting to stay in a luxurious historic home was an amazing experience. Up until she'd rented her most recent apartment, Hannah had only lived in places that were aged. Leaky faucets and questionable electric had been part of her growing-up experience.

"There's a robe in the closet, if you'd like to wear it. That way you don't have to get dressed when you come outside."

She made a quick stop in the bathroom and used a luxury moisture-rich cleansing bar for her face. Now she was going to need to buy these for her place since she'd discovered she liked being pampered.

When she exited, he was standing near the window, and

he turned to look at her.

Unable to help herself, she froze and stared at him.

He was wearing navy-colored boxer briefs. Until now, she hadn't seen his mostly naked body.

His arm muscles were massive, thicker than she'd thought they would be. Why it was a surprise, she didn't know. When he'd taken off his tuxedo jacket at the club, she'd known he had a nice build, with broad shoulders and a slim waist. He'd picked her up and carried her.

His chest had a scattering of hair that arrowed down his breathtakingly sexy abs to disappear inside the waistband of his tight underwear. Beneath them, his cock was hard.

She shook her head and ordered herself to get a grip, leave the bedroom and brew the coffee, but she was unable to move. Instead, she was drinking in his muscular and powerful legs, thinking of his strength as he held her down and fucked her.

"See something you like?"

"I..."

His lips quirked.

Warmth flooded her, a combination of embarrassment and arousal. But then, instead of denial, she opted for the truth. He'd been vocal in his appreciation of her. "Yes, I do. Sir."

"So do I, Hannah."

As if hypnotized by him, she walked toward him.

"I'm looking forward to spending the day with you. I have a number of ideas of how we can fill the time."

Even though he'd satisfied her again and again, she was suddenly ravenous—wanting her fantasies to become a reality. "Sorry I was so tired last night. I thought we might... Well. I mean, I assumed..."

"That we'd have sex? It was my plan, yes."

"I didn't mean for you to be unsatisfied."

"Did I give you that idea?" He demolished the distance between them. "If so, it was unintentional." He brushed back the hair from her face, and his voice resonated with tenderness, and then, when he spoke again, a hint of teasing. "If I'm honest, I'm rather proud of myself that I wore you out so completely. You passed out in about twenty seconds."

Because he was relaxed, he put her at ease.

"Today, though, I fully intend to set a different pace." He lowered his hand, and her gaze was riveted on him as he trailed his fingers down her chest, to trace the globe of her breasts before circling her nipples. They'd hardened even before he touched them through the T-shirt. "You're not wearing panties, are you?"

"Ah…"

"Oh?" he arched an eyebrow as he caught her gaze.

"I am. Sir."

"That was a mistake."

At odds with his words, there was no displeasure in his tone. Was he pleased that she'd violated an unspoken rule?

"I presume that won't happen again?"

"Of course not, Sir."

He stopped touching her.

"I assume you want me to take them off now." *While you watch?* He didn't need to answer. His eyes darkened, and that was all the response she needed for her to reach beneath the T-shirt and remove her thong.

"The color is nice," he said when the scrap of material landed on the floor.

Her tote contained a few different choices. When she'd gone to the lingerie store, they'd had a special on panties, so she'd bought a dozen, in all different colors, some with lace, others that were plain. "It matches the rope you used last night." She'd selected them on purpose.

"Seems we're both deliberate with our choices. I wanted

something that contrasted well, your pale skin with red marks."

He made her senses swim.

"Show me."

She slowly turned and drew up her T-shirt again. Then she spread her legs and bent to grant him access to every part of her body.

"Such perfect behavior. Makes me want to take you, hard."

She was drenched from the sound of his need. "Do it. Please." She glanced back at him. "Yes."

"I'd planned something a little more romantic."

But this was perfect. She wasn't looking for seduction. She was looking for new memories. "Take me."

He crossed to the nightstand and grabbed a condom.

Fascinated, she watched him remove his underwear. And then she saw the size of his erect cock and gulped a shallow breath. He was huge, and when he took her bent over, the penetration would be shockingly deep. If last night hadn't happened, she might doubt her ability to do this at all.

It took him mere seconds to open the package and roll the latex down his length.

He stopped in front of her, and for a moment she was nervous that he'd ask her to suck on his massive dick.

Instead, with a grin, he instructed her to wet his fingers. "But don't think you're off the hook. You will take me that way later."

Filled with butterflies, she sucked. His pseudo-threat had temporarily replaced arousal with fear.

"I'll never ask you to do something that's impossible, Hannah."

She might believe him, if his cock wasn't jutting in front of her.

When his fingers were wet, he moved behind her to play

with her clit.

It took him only a couple of strokes to make her knees weaken. He seemed to know her body better than anyone ever had, and it was difficult for her to remember that they were new lovers.

He dipped inside her. "Sore?"

"Not exactly. It's more like I'm tender, Sir."

"It's a good thing your ass and mouth are both available for me, then, isn't it?"

Now that she'd seen him naked, her fear was a very real thing.

"You skin is unblemished. Not a single mark is left over from last night. Pity." He slapped her right ass cheek.

Shrieking from shock, not pain, she rocked forward.

"And that position, Hannah, is even better. Try to stay there."

"I thought you weren't going to ask the impossible."

"Well, not often," he amended. "Ten times a day, perhaps."

When his cockhead was against her, she tensed and almost broke position, but he curled his fingers into one of her hip bones to keep her in place.

"Turn your toes in a little."

He slowly worked part of himself inside her. "Relax for me." He reached beneath her to flick a finger across her clit, making her cry out and wiggle. And that was enough for him to surge forward, claiming her completely.

With him so deep, against her womb, she could hardly breathe. Instead of fucking her, he remained still, allowing her to accommodate his length.

"You're built for me, Hannah." He played with her nipples, gently tweaking and squeezing, his touch so light that it drove her mad.

It wasn't consistent enough to heighten her arousal. Instead, it left her needy. And then, he tugged on one, and lightning shot through her. *"Yes."* All of a sudden, she was wet again, and her body was supple.

"That's better."

He fucked her in earnest then, replacing thought with sensation. Nothing existed except him.

Mason gripped her waist, keeping her where he wanted her but also supporting her body. She had nothing to worry about, and he allowed her to surrender to the moment.

"I could fuck you all day."

All she knew was that she wanted him inside her. "Oh Mason!"

"Do you want to come?"

"Please."

He continued to relentlessly impale her and, with his silence, withhold his permission.

Now that the urge to orgasm was uncoiling, she could think of nothing else. His masculine scent filled her. His calluses abraded her skin. Mason's breathing was as labored as her own, and still he rode her.

"Sir! *Sir..."* Unexpectedly, the climax rushed through her, and she screamed his name.

He moved in short thrusts, drawing out the orgasm even longer.

When she was depleted, he was there. He pulled out, then moved her to the bed. "I'll finish you off this way." Mason knelt, then took a moment to be sure she was properly lubricated before stroking himself a few times.

She sighed as he sank into her.

This position was much easier, and when all of him was inside her, she realized he was studying her. His eyes were flinty, hiding his thoughts.

"Put your arms above your head."

When she did, he clamped her wrists.

"This..." He fucked her but never released her gaze or his

grip. "You..."

Unbelievably, the conviction in his words brought her back to the cusp. His cock swelled. He rode her until she cried out. And then, only then, did he allow himself to come.

"That was..."

He kissed her, with complete sweetness. He was dichotomy, toughness and tenderness in the same moment.

"Yes," he agreed. "It was." He rolled to one side but tucked her into the nook of his arm while they both drowsed.

A few minutes later, after stroking her shoulder with the gentlest of touches, he left the bed.

Lazily, she propped herself on an arm to watch him.

He stopped to pick up her thong. "If I liked you in underwear, I would have approved of them."

With a grin, she flopped back onto the pillow.

Right now, she was replete. Having sex with him, submitting to his dominance, had been spectacular. With each moment, Liam's powerful effect on her was fading.

The tiniest possible part of her wished the weekend with Mason would never end. The practical part of her, however, was relieved that they had a time limit. It would be far too easy to fall for him.

In the beginning, Liam had been kind as well. Once he'd fastened a collar around her neck, things had changed. Instead of caring, he'd become possessive, seeing her as an extension of himself. Everything she did reflected on him. He required perfection, and she never met his exacting standards. Incrementally, over a year, he'd become lost in his power, determined to bend her to his will. Her life had become a series of recriminations to go along with his punishments.

To protect herself from another disaster, she needed to avoid giving away her heart along with her body.

Why did Mason have to be so damn tempting?

CHAPTER 7

Shoving aside the sudden uncertainty that was gnawing at her, Hannah climbed out of bed and pulled Mason's T-shirt on. Since she was going to be busy in the kitchen, she opted not to wear a robe.

The spicy scent of his soap filled the air, and she fought against the impulse to go into the bathroom and join him. She was pretty certain he wouldn't object, but it would bind them closer, and she'd just vowed not to do that.

She scooped up her discarded thong, then placed it in her tote bag before leaving the room and closing the door behind her.

Instead of going straight downstairs, she decided to explore the home's second story. He had a guest room, with another four-poster bed. And there was another bathroom, much smaller than his, without a bathtub, but with an oversize walk-in shower. It, too, had cozy touches, candles, round cakes of soap, luxurious towels, a teak bench. The sink was glass, and the faucet would flow like a waterfall. Nearby, a vase contained fresh-cut white carnations.

When she fled from Liam, she'd done so suddenly. The

need to get out was immediate, and it had demanded action. There was no way she could go through that kind of experience again.

Fiona had caught the first available flight to Austin. While Liam was at work, they rented a truck, packed up Hannah's belongings, and locked the door on their way out.

It wasn't until now that she realized she'd been living such a utilitarian life. Because she left so many things behind and the deposit and first month's rent had wiped out her savings, she bought many items secondhand. Only her bed, sheets, blankets, and bathroom linens were new.

Her savings had been rebuilt, but she hadn't focused on making her place homier.

Living in this luxury was eye-opening and addictive.

And because of it, she would always remember this weekend. And *him.*

That thought was an unwelcome intrusion.

A room at the end of the hallway served as a home gym, with yoga mats, free weights, an elliptical machine, even a treadmill. A large mirror took up most of the far wall. Maybe she could grab a chair and watch him pump his muscles. With the mirror, she would be able to see every part of him.

Shaking her head at her fantasy, she peeked inside his home office. The walls had a few pictures of framed magazine covers and homes that she assumed his company had built.

It seemed he placed his personal mementos in his bedroom.

Behind a door, a narrow, curved set of stairs led to a third level. From the outside, the home appeared to be a two-story, so she guessed there was an attic, rather than bedrooms, up there.

When the water that had been rushing suddenly stopped,

she headed down the stairs, holding on to the polished banister.

Over the years, how many children had slid down it, only to be admonished by a parent? Even she was tempted to give it a try.

In the kitchen, she found the coffee and filters. After setting the machine to brew, she found her bag and pulled out her phone.

The red notification light blinked rapidly, so she scrolled to the message window. There was a text from Fiona.

Is it possible to die from boredom?

Hannah grinned. Since the message had been sent before eleven, maybe the evening had gotten better.

She scrolled to the second one.

For the love of God, tell me you're having fun. One of us should be.

Then another had arrived at one a.m.

Call me when you can. I want all the details.

After responding, asking her friend if she was awake, Hannah rummaged through the kitchen, looking for something to make for breakfast.

For a bachelor who didn't cook, the pantry and refrigerator were generously stocked. She found a bag of croissants in the bread bin. Then, inspired, she sought out eggs and cheese.

Working in here, with so much room, and high-end knives, was a dream. She hummed as she sliced the croissants, then popped them in the oven to warm. As she was whisking salt and pepper into her scrambled egg mixture, Fiona's ringtone—a high-energy mambo—spilled through the silence.

Hannah answered on speakerphone. "Did your evening get better?"

"Tell me this, girlfriend. Why am I up so early on a Saturday?"

"I'll take that as a no. What went wrong?"

"He keeps asking if he's being a good Dom. Reassuring him and trying to guide him along the way tuckered me out."

Hannah turned on a burner and placed a frying pan on it.

"But Lord have mercy, that's not the worst. He snores. Like a machine gun, only louder. These stuttering, awful inhalations. Girl, I'm telling you, he's so obnoxious I can still hear him, and I'm outside."

"Can you get out of the contract for the weekend?"

"I probably could." Fiona hesitated. "But I don't want to. I feel kind of sorry for him."

Hannah added a dollop of sweet butter to the pan and let it melt before pouring in the eggs. "Sorry for him?"

When Fiona replied, there was compassion in her words. "You know, maybe he's not actually a jerk. Maybe he's just insecure?"

"That's a possibility." She stirred the eggs. "I still think you like him."

Fiona sighed. "He's...sweet. Nice."

"And you're not looking for sweet?" Hannah surmised.

"I didn't think so."

"You like him!"

"Get out of here. He snores! And..."

Shocked, Hannah dropped the spatula. Fiona constantly flitted from Dom to Dom, seeking something newer, brighter, shinier. So the confusion in her voice was stunning. "You like him," Hannah repeated with more force.

"I— No. That's enough about me. I've been pestering you because I want the scoop on One Night Dom."

Afraid of Mason overhearing his unflattering nickname, she snatched up the phone, turned off the speaker. She glanced around, just to make sure he wasn't there.

"Amazing, right?"

"He was. He is."

"I'm so envious right now, I could turn green. You're lucky that's a bad color for me."

Hannah laughed.

"Seriously, I'm happy for you. You're okay?"

Sore. Tender. Satisfied. And craving more. She settled for, "Yes." Physically. As long as she could steer him away from probing questions, she'd get through the weekend and be happy for the experience.

"Listen, I gotta go. Mr. Snorebox is headed my way."

"Try to have a good time."

"I'll forgive a lot of sins if he takes me out to breakfast."

Fiona's relentless optimism was one of the things Hannah appreciated the most about her friend.

Still grinning after the call ended, Hannah pulled the baking tray from the oven, then layered scrambled eggs onto the bottom halves of the croissants before adding shredded cheese. She put the tops in place, then used a potholder to slide the rack back into place before closing the door and setting the timer.

Between the coffee and the bread, the kitchen smelled delicious, and her stomach rumbled, spurring her to find a tray.

Hannah grabbed a bowl for sliced strawberries, then poured herself a large cup of coffee. After adding a huge splash of cream, she took the first fortifying sip.

With her eyes closed, she leaned against the countertop, utterly content.

At first, she didn't recognize the feeling. She'd spent so long being unsettled, expecting Liam to find her or come after her, that caution had become a part of her life. Even after she heard he had a new submissive, she hadn't let her guard down.

"A penny for your thoughts?"

Hannah jolted, almost spilling her coffee. With a trembling hand, she placed the cup on the counter beside her.

"Sorry. Didn't mean to startle you. I wasn't being quiet."

Save me. Mason looked so damn sexy that her heart lurched. His dark blond hair was wet, and his bare chest was dotted with droplets of water. He wore black shorts that did nothing to disguise his erection.

How was that even possible? They'd already had mind-blowing sex.

His legs spread wide, he studied her, his jade eyes narrowed, as if wanting to see past her personality to explore the essence of who she was. He unnerved her. "Coffee?" She pushed away from the counter. "It may not be as strong as you say yours is, but it should do the job."

"Thanks."

She grabbed a big, sturdy mug with his company logo on it. "I'm guessing cream. No sugar."

"Astute."

"Not really." She smiled. "Since you don't cook, there's not a lot of reason for you to have an open container of cream in the refrigerator. And if you used sugar, it would be accessible instead of tucked somewhere at the back of a shelf.

"I shall dub thee Super Sleuth."

She grinned as she poured the brew into the cup, then slid the cream toward him. He made it impossible for her to keep an emotional wall between them.

"Can I help you with anything?"

"I made some croissant sandwiches."

"Is that what I smell? When I was in the shower, I was hallucinating that I was at my favorite breakfast restaurant."

"That's a good thing, I hope."

"Yeah. Very good." Though he accepted the mug from her, he didn't take a drink or move away. He'd planted himself so that he was very much in the middle of her work area.

"Should only be a few minutes. I thought I'd slice some strawberries to go with them."

"Slice? Is that what you're supposed to do with them?"

She laughed. "Or eat them whole, I suppose."

"That's fine with me."

"I was planning on drowning them in cream."

"Even better."

He took a drink of his coffee, then saluted her. "You can be in charge. Though it pains me to admit it, this is better than mine."

"You're an appreciative audience." She wrinkled her nose as she studied him. "Or a crafty one who likes me doing all the kitchen things."

His grin sent her into a freefall. "An appreciative one. Without a doubt."

He sat at the counter where he could watch her work.

After washing the berries and patting them dry, she placed them in the bowl and added the cream. "I was going to bring the tray upstairs. I thought we might eat outside before it gets too hot."

He nodded. "I enjoy watching the comings and goings in the neighborhood. Kids playing. The guy across the street has been teaching his son to ride a bike. After he fell last week, the training wheels went back on. Mom and the kid seemed happy. But I saw Shawn take them off a couple of days ago, while his kid was inside. I'm guessing they'll be trying again this morning." Mason grinned.

That he took so much delight in a small pleasure charmed her.

The timer beeped, and she pulled out their breakfast. "I made you two. I figured you had an appetite."

"You should have made yourself two." He took a drink. "You're going to need the energy."

How did he do that to her? Make her want to fall to her knees without even asking?

While she transferred the sandwiches onto the plates, he refilled their drinks. "Do you want me to carry the tray?"

"That would be awesome." Someone to share the load. She grabbed the coffees and followed him upstairs and through the bedroom. He placed the tray on the dresser long enough to open the window.

"This is weird."

"You're supposed to walk through doors, right?"

"Yes."

"Windows are aesthetically pleasing as well as practical."

Once they were outside, he put the tray on a small table, and she placed the cups near it. Moments later, he flicked a switch to activate the overhead fan before heading inside to pull on a short-sleeve T-shirt.

When he returned, he took a seat on the small wicker couch. There was plenty of room next to him, but she opted to sit in a chair that was at a slight angle to him.

"I scare you."

"Sandwich?" She picked up a plate and offered it to him.

"That was an artful dodge."

She smiled. "Strawberries?"

"I'll take the hint." He accepted the plate and took a bite of the croissant. "This is better than eating out."

"Glad you like it." The bread was the perfect combination of crispy on the outside and warm on the inside. The cheese had melted into the eggs, so the entire thing was buttery and filling.

"Tell me we have enough for tomorrow morning as well."

"We may have to go shopping."

"There's a market a few blocks away. We can go later."

Grocery shopping? She glanced down at her plate to scoop up a piece that had flaked off her croissant. That hadn't been part of her plan. She'd been thinking sex and submission, not relationship-type of activities.

A breeze rustled through the trees, and she sat back to relax. "It is pleasant out here."

"Kind of day that makes people fall in love with the Crescent City."

"Then comes August and September." She selected a strawberry, then sucked the cream off it before biting it in half. "You were right. Leaving them whole was a better choice than slicing them," she admitted.

"Stick with me, Hannah. I'll show you all the good things."

"I think that might be true."

His grin was quick and a little too triumphant.

Just then, a dad and a young boy walked out onto the street, pushing a bicycle.

"No training wheels," Mason observed.

A woman followed—the mom presumably. She checked the strap of her son's helmet and adjusted one of his elbow pads. "I had no helmet. No pads," he mused.

The dad glanced up at them and shook his head.

Hannah smiled.

The woman stepped back and lifted her cell phone.

Judging by the way she continued to hold it steady, she was filming the today's attempt.

The dad held on to the seat and handlebars and shouted, "Pedal!"

They took off down the street, dad at a run, the bike wobbling frantically. Dad let go. "You got it! Pedal!"

The boy looked back and promptly fell over.

"Good life lesson, right?" Mason asked. "Don't look back. Keep moving forward. Get back on and try again."

Maybe for others. She wanted to be sure she never fell again.

The mom took off running to check on her child.

Down the street, the dad stood the bike up again. "Pedal, son! Keep moving!" Dad ran alongside the bike, and then, right after he let go, another crash happened.

She and Mason watched for a minute before she returned her attention to him. "You were going to tell me more about the house."

"The old beauty was in disrepair. But my dad fell in love." For a moment, he hesitated. His eyes clouded like they had last night when he'd picked up the picture of his father from the mantelpiece. "He wanted it for my mom, as a surprise. I think for him, it wasn't about status—it was about giving her something beautiful because she deserved it. She married him when he wasn't making a lot of money, when the construction industry was in a downturn. Her parents helped them buy a bungalow, but as far as I know, it bothered him that he hadn't been able to provide that for her."

Mason slid his empty plate back onto the tray and reached for his coffee mug. "Anyway. In his early years, he'd had a paper route, and he'd delivered to this street. He remembered the history. About five years ago, it came on the market as a foreclosure. Nothing was up to code. Basically it was uninhabitable. But Dad was enchanted. He had this gift for seeing the possible.

He became obsessed with researching the history. Fortunately a bunch of it existed, original drawings, and a magazine feature."

"The one that's framed downstairs?"

He nodded. "As you might have noticed, the original structure was built with Grecian columns, which are more square. Sometime later, they were replaced by Corinthian ones, like you see now. The wrought iron fell into disrepair sometime in the twentieth century, and an unknown owner replaced it with wood. Dad couldn't stop thinking about it, so he negotiated a deal with the bank. It took months before the deal closed." He looked off into the distance. Not at the activity in the street, but somewhere unseeing. "The house was all he could talk about. And then he got the diagnosis."

"Oh God, Mason."

"He kept going but needed help. He was supposed to have years ahead of him. It turned out he had less than one." The pain made his voice waver. "We worked on it together every day. At night, we'd sit on ladders or the stripped floors and share a whiskey while we made plans that never happened."

"I'm so very sorry for your loss." It had to have destroyed him.

"So I finished it." He shrugged. "The irony? Mom never wanted this house. Her tastes are simpler. She likes the bungalow where I grew up. It was her home. That's where the memories are, Christmases, birthdays. First day of kindergarten, homecomings, prom, graduation parties. Learning to ride a bike." He chuckled. "She was happy in the bungalow and didn't want to move. So I made some changes to the plans for this house to increase the resale value."

"But you haven't been able to part with it."

He shrugged. "While finishing the renovation, I moved in. And then..."

"Like your dad, you fell in love?"

"Never meant to. But there's something about it. I found a hundred reasons not to sell. The location is perfect. Plenty of room for my home office and a workshop out back. Investment potential. I'm too busy to look for something else. Mom sold the house to me, and I made a few changes to suit me."

"I don't blame you."

"Except for the fact it's better suited for a family than a bachelor." He shrugged.

She finished her coffee, then looked over at him. "So, I have a question for you." One that had bothered her since yesterday. "Turnabout is fair play."

"True enough."

"Last night, you asked me why I wanted to be in the auction. But I'm curious why you participated. Do you do it every year?" What was he hoping to get out of it? Have a submissive without the obligation of a long-term relationship?

"Until Thursday night, I never planned to attend."

She sat back. "Really?"

"Aviana—Mistress Aviana—is on the board of Reclamation."

"The charity the auction was for?"

"One and the same. You may not know that my father started it."

"Really?"

"I'm the current president," he went on. "Aviana is more than generous with her time and resources. For the past two years I skipped the event. I sent money, sizable amounts, actually. But that doesn't equal support for the event, and she let me know that."

It was interesting, seeing Aviana as more than a BDSM club owner and kick-ass Domme. And Mason as a son, caretaker of his father's dreams. "Because you're president, you had no choice."

"That's an accurate summarization."

Hannah curled up in the chair and waited for him to go on.

"I had no intention of bidding on a submissive." He paused a second, as if choosing his words. "And then I saw you."

Now-familiar skitters shimmied through her.

"Beauty. Elegance."

She blushed. Those words didn't seem to apply to her.

"Nervousness."

That definitely fit her.

"Distrust, even."

Once again, he knew things about her that others didn't.

"You looked at me, Hannah."

She went still. He couldn't know that. The spotlights had been blazing, and there were at least a hundred people in the room.

"You chose me as much as I chose you." He leaned forward. "The question is why. You don't know me."

Hannah debated her answer. Denial? Tell him the truth? Or something close to it? "You seemed safe."

"In what way?"

"Doms—subs, I'm sure, also—get reputations." She wasn't going to reveal his nickname. "You're known for being a good Dom. Satisfying your submissive."

He raised an eyebrow so fast she knew he didn't believe her.

She moved positions completely, reversing directions in the chair. "You scene with a lot of different women."

Her statement didn't dissuade him from his questions. "You were looking for a man who doesn't want a commitment?"

Being honest here was harmless enough. "Of course."

"A weekend, nothing more. You don't even live in the same city. That grants you a certain amount of anonymity, doesn't it? We aren't going to run into each other in town or at the club."

She lifted a shoulder.

He propped his elbows on his knees. "Does this have anything to do with the fact that you hate collars? Being left alone."

She dug her fingers into the seat cushion.

"Fuck." He jumped up to pace the gallery.

She remained where she was.

A minute later, maybe more, he stopped in front of her. "Humiliation?"

"Please…" Except for one night, about six months after she'd left Liam, Hannah had never talked about this.

Mason plowed a hand into his hair. "I'm safe. That's what you said, right? Because you only have to commit to two nights. And you're pretty damn sure I'm not going to ask for anything else."

"We have an agreement."

He expelled a jagged sigh. "He fucking hurt you."

"More emotionally than anything."

"Don't. Just don't. Okay?" Mason dropped into his seat. "Don't negate it. If you didn't agree, there's no consent. No one should tolerate that. Relationships are about taking care of each other, being there, supporting, understanding. And not ever about pain."

Pretending she wasn't affected by his insight, she picked up her cup of coffee. It was cold and almost impossible to swallow past the knot in her throat.

"I get it. I hate it. But I'm glad you chose me."

She wasn't sure whether or not she was. He was so much more complicated than she'd bargained for. Specifically she wanted him because he would spank her, maybe tie her up, but never pry into her personal life.

Across the street, the little boy threw his leg over the crossbar and settled onto the seat again. Dad leaned in to grab the seat and hold it steady. "Ready? Pedal!"

About twenty steps later, Dad let go and grabbed his knees, huffing for breath. "Keep going!"

Leaning forward with incredible focus, the boy turned the wheels ferociously.

The dad raised his hands to clap but dropped them right away, obviously afraid of breaking the magic.

"It's a good lesson," Mason repeated. "Keep going. Don't look back."

Hannah wasn't sure she could do that. Especially now that she knew so much more about Mason, how deep he was, how completely he loved, how he relentlessly continued to dig for answers she didn't want to give. Losing her heart to him would destroy her completely.

CHAPTER 8

Mason's phone rang. He'd ignore it in favor of another cup of coffee on the porch with Hannah, except for the fact that he recognized the ringtone. "It's my mother." If he didn't answer, she wouldn't leave a message, but she would call again and again until he finally picked up.

"You should talk to her. I'll clean up the dishes."

"I'll be right back." He stood. "No need to hurry. We have strawberries to finish." And they weren't done with their conversation, either.

By the time he picked up the mobile device from the dresser, it had stopped ringing.

While Hannah had been making breakfast, he sent texts canceling the meetings he had scheduled for the day. He also asked one of his site managers to drop by their renovation in Algiers. There was a scheduled walk-through with the homeowners to update progress and set the completion date.

In addition to missing his mother's call, Mason hadn't seen the response from his manager, Bruce. Seemed he had his kids for the day, and the oldest had a baseball game this afternoon.

Standing where he could watch Hannah move to the swing and set it in motion, he pressed the button to dial his mom.

"Mason, darling..."

He braced for impact. She didn't call him darling unless she wanted something. "Morning, Mom."

"Norman and I were wondering..."

Hannah tipped back her head, and her sleep-tousled hair fell in appealing waves behind her, making him want to fist it as he held her prisoner for his kiss.

"Are you listening, son?"

"Sorry. Distracted." *Obsessed.*

"It's for sale by owner."

He blinked. "What is?"

She sighed with impatience. "The house I want you to look at. Norman thinks it would be a good investment for me."

As if she needed any more investments, or advice from her new man. "Start over, please."

"John called this morning."

John Thoroughgood had been a longtime financial adviser to their family. Now that this wasn't about a random suggestion from Norman, Mason was more interested. "Okay."

"He has a client who has had a slight downturn in circumstances."

Polite for he's broke as hell.

"He was evidently partway through restoring a home near the French Quarter to be used as a vacation rental before he ran out of funds."

"You sure you're up for a vacation rental? That's a lot of effort unless you hire it out."

"It could be a long-term lease, perhaps. Or we can flip it."

He blinked. "Flip it?"

"You know, like on the shows. You invest some money and then sell it for a lot more."

Mason shook his head, glad they weren't on a video chat. He knew what a flip was. Honestly, he was surprised his mom did. In all the years his dad had been in the business, she'd shown no interest in his work.

"We have an appointment at eleven." She recited an address on Kerlerec. "Can you meet us there?"

"I'll be there."

"Thank you, darling."

After sending a text to his manager, Mason placed his phone upside down on the dresser, then went back outside. Even though he didn't have an invitation, he sat next to Hannah on the swing. Slowly, with a smile, she lifted her head.

"Morning, again." Being this close to her was pleasant. She smelled of sweetness and sex. He couldn't get enough. He curled a lock of her hair around his finger. "As much as I'd like to spend the entire day fucking you until you can't walk, duty calls."

"Oh? Something for your mom?"

"She's looking at a house. Well, her and Norman. And probably her financial adviser. It will be a party. Then I have a walkthrough with a HO—sorry, homeowner—to go over their renovations and discuss their budget." He shrugged. "I tried to pass off the responsibility, but my manager is busy with his kids."

"That's fine. I can hang out here or go back to Fiona's for the afternoon. Or grab lunch at my favorite restaurant."

"I prefer you come with me."

She angled her body to better see him. "Won't that be awkward? With your mom? And I'm sure the homeowners won't want me tagging along."

In all his years dating Deborah, he had never invited her

to go with him. "It will be fine, and I think you might enjoy it, since you've asked so many questions about this house."

"I would. Have fun, I mean."

"Good. We're meeting Mom at eleven. Which gives you time for a leisurely bath. And you're going to need it."

She shivered. "Is that so…"

For a moment, Hannah hesitated, as if she was deciding how to address him. When he'd placed the winning bid, he'd told her he didn't want to be called Master, saying that the word spoke of commitment and responsibility. But now he longed to hear the term of respect roll off her tongue. And he wanted to deserve the title.

In the silence, she finished her sentence. "Sir?"

"Assuredly, sub." He tugged his finger from her hair and shoved away his unexpected angst. "I suggest you get your hot little ass inside before I strip you right here."

"You wouldn't!"

"Try me," he suggested. It might help him vanquish the unsettled feelings slithering inside him.

"But the neighbors—"

"It would be quite the talk of the town, wouldn't it? You naked, bent over the wrought iron?"

She stood so abruptly, the swing wobbled.

Mason narrowed his eyes wickedly. "I wish you'd made the other decision."

"I'll bet you do." Hannah dashed inside the house before he could hurry her along with a spank. Happier than he had a right to be, he followed. Mason pulled the tieback so that the curtain closed, but he left the window open. "Take off your shirt."

Her gaze on him, she did as he said. Like the perfect submissive, she'd followed his instructions and skipped undergarments.

When she was naked, he pointed at a spot in front of him. "On your knees, Hannah."

She reached out a hand as if to steady herself. "I'm not sure—"

"You'll manage."

Even though she wrinkled her nose to express her doubts, she complied with his command.

God, he loved having her in this position, her mouth so close to his crotch. "Remove my shorts and then place your hands behind your neck."

Her hands were warm on his skin, and the moment he was free of the constricting clothing, his cock jutted forward.

"Sir..."

Slowly, she adjusted herself to the position he'd instructed. "Good. Now open your mouth for me."

Instead of instantly responding, she closed her eyes.

He chuckled. "That's not going to make sucking my cock any easier." He placed his palms on either side of her head to hold her in place.

A frantic pulse beat in her throat, but she glanced up at him. "Uhm, may I touch you?"

"Of course. I'd like that. "

Hannah curled one hand around his cock and laid her other palm on the back of his thigh. Had anything ever been more perfect?

Slowly she leaned toward him, and when she was close enough, she licked him.

"Mmm."

Goddamn. What she did to him. Other women had sucked his dick, but no one had made that thrilling sound of approval when they'd tasted his precum.

After a shallow breath, she licked his perineum, then closed her mouth around his cockhead.

Unthinkingly, he tightened his grip on her.

"Oh, Sir." She took a short break to catch her breath, then licked and sucked again. Then she began stroking and taking more of him, going lower and lower on his shaft.

When most of him was in her mouth, she gagged and pulled away.

"You're doing well."

She wiped tears from her eyes but gave him a tremulous smile before continuing on.

With little moans, she worked her mouth around him, enthusiastically, rather than from duty. Then she took hold of his balls.

Fucking hell. Still gripping her, he tilted his head and gave himself over to her. She was feminine perfection. Mason savored every moment.

His dick throbbed with need, and his balls tightened in her grip.

He was seconds away from spilling himself down her throat, and he had no intention of doing so. "Stop." She continued, and he repeated himself. It was supposed to be a forceful order, but it emerged as a guttural plea.

Mason captured her chin and gave it a gentle squeeze. "Stop, Hannah."

Slowly, she pulled away to sit on her haunches. "Did I do something wrong?"

"No. That's not possible." So he didn't go off like a rocket, he avoided touching himself. "Stand up, please." He offered his hand to assist her, and she accepted.

But it wasn't enough for him. He scooped her from the floor. With a yelp, she wrapped her legs around his waist as he carried her across the room to the bed to unceremoniously dump her on the mattress.

She started to scramble away, but he grabbed hold of her ankle and yanked her back. Then he pulled her to where he wanted her, right on the edge.

"Mason!"

He imprisoned her, clamping his palms on her slender legs, right above her knees. Then he spread her legs wide.

"Oh Sir!"

"Play with your nipples." He buried his head between her thighs.

"You're not—"

He licked her pussy and inserted two fingers inside her as he pressed against her clitoris.

She arched as she struggled to escape.

"I'll slap your naughty little cunt if you don't stay still."

His threat made her freeze for a second, but when he slid his fingers back and forth, she thrashed about.

Mason flicked his tongue, making her cry out his name.

When his fingers were drenched with her arousal, he withdrew them and slipped one of them into her ass.

"Yes, yes! No! I can't…" She wailed.

Tonguing her faster, he entered her ass with the second finger and fucked her relentlessly.

"Mason! Sir! Master…I'm going to come."

He pulled out and pushed away from her.

"No," she protested.

"We need to get moving." Mason released his clamplike grip and stood.

"You're going to leave me like this?" She worked her way up onto her elbows. "Really?"

"Like…?"

"Hanging?"

"It's both of us, Miss Hannah. Ensuring we'll be anxious to return home."

She dropped her head back onto the mattress with dramatic flair. "I must protest your ghastly behavior, Sir."

"So noted." He grinned.

"How about if I beg?"

"Please do."

She narrowed her gaze. "But it wouldn't work, right? You have no intention of changing your mind."

"None whatsoever. But I could spank you for arguing with your Dom." That threat was empty. If he spanked her, he'd fuck her and get her off. And that would defeat his purpose. "You're running out of time to take a bath."

He loomed over her, placing his palms flat on the bed, on either side of her body. Then he pinched one of her nipples. When it hardened, he pulled on it. The scent of her immediately filled the air. The power he had over her responses was heady. "You have two choices. I can finish you off here and now."

"But...?"

"If I do, it will be your last orgasm of the day. Since I'm planning on scening with you again and again, I'll deny you for"—he looked away while pretending to do the math—"fifteen hours. Oh, and I won't be giving you any opportunity to sneak one in."

"I've heard you're one of the best Doms on the planet."

"That, lovely Hannah, is a lie and a terrible attempt at appealing to my ego." He grinned at her ineffective attempt, then sucked on the nipple he'd tormented. He bit and laved it with attention until she writhed beneath him.

"Please? Please, Mason."

Then he released her and left her. At the door to the bathroom, he looked back. "On second thought, perhaps you are right. The best Doms keep their subs guessing and on the edge."

She groaned. Or perhaps it was a moan. At either rate, it was the delicious sound of distress—one he enjoyed tremendously.

~

"Would you like me to wait in the car?"

"No." Near the property where they were meeting his mother, Mason slid the gearshift into *park* and studied Hannah. "Do you want to?"

"It seems a little strange to meet your Mom, I guess." She toyed with her purse strap. "But I'm interested to see the house."

So was he.

Before leaving home he'd done a search on the address. The most recent pictures were a couple of years old, when the house was sold as is. It was a 1918 Creole-style cottage that had been abandoned. Floors were missing boards. Windows were shattered. Shingles were missing from the roof, which meant water damage. No doubt it needed new plumbing and electric. Probably required heat and air-conditioning, as well. Since the owner had started renovations, perhaps some of it had been brought up to code.

Judging by the peeling paint on the outside, not much.

But still…

"It has some charm, doesn't it?" she asked.

He glanced over at her. "You see it?"

"Maybe paint it a bright color. Plant some lush foliage. It's a good size lot, compared to the others around it. Restore the porch. Oh! Maybe add a fan. And shutters. They'd totally add charm."

Good for a storm, and aesthetics. He nodded.

His mother and Norman arrived, so Mason shut off the car engine. "Ready?"

Hannah nodded, but her fingers were tight on her purse strap.

He came around to the passenger side to help her from the vehicle. "She won't bite." He leaned forward to speak against her ear. "But I might."

Her eyes widened, but he'd jolted her from her nerves.

"Mason!" his mother greeted, kissing his cheek. "And who have we here?" She scowled. "You didn't tell me you were bringing company."

"Mom, this is Hannah Gill. Hannah, I'd like you to meet my mother, Judith."

"A pleasure, Mrs. Sullivan. Mason has said some very nice things about you."

"Call me Judith, dear. I like you already."

In his mom's customary way, she swept Hannah into a huge hug while Mason shook hands with Norman.

Just then, Thoroughgood pulled alongside a curb and began the painful-looking process of squeezing himself out of the electric vehicle that was about the size of an enclosed motorcycle. The man could afford the priciest automobiles in existence, but he chose the most economical option possible.

Once he was upright, and twice as tall as the car was high, he straightened his rumpled blazer. It was circa 1970, with leather patches on the elbows.

Instead of shaking Mason's hand, Thoroughgood pulled him into a bone-crushing hug.

"And who are you, young lady?" He glanced at Hannah then shot Mason a sly look.

"Hannah Gill," she introduced herself. "And if I'm not mistaken…you played for the Saints."

He pulled back his head, as if impressed. "Five seasons, ma'am."

Mason was stunned as well.

"You were a first round draft choice. Played college ball for LSU."

Thoroughgood squinted his eyes at Mason. "You told her?"

"Not one word. I promise. She's a bona fide fan."

"Well, Ms. Gill. You're my new favorite person. Now let's get out of this heat before we all expire."

Since the front steps were missing, Norman and Mason helped his mother up. Then Mason took Hannah by the waist and lifted her off her feet, turning her to place her on the porch.

Not wanting to release her, he held on for a very long time.

Thoroughgood entered the code to the lockbox that contained the key. Rather than waiting for them, he shut the door.

"That was impressive," Mason said.

"I love football. And he's a legend, right? Meeting him is a dream. Just…thank you." She kissed his forehead.

And he was fucking hooked on her.

His mother opened the door and peeked her head out. "Are you two coming?"

"Right behind you," he assured her.

The inside matched the pictures he'd seen online. But it was mostly cosmetic.

"Electric's new," Thoroughgood said. "Plumbing. Roof."

The basics.

"Air-conditioning."

"Thank all the mercies for that!" his mother exclaimed.

Though the square footage wasn't impressive, as Hannah had said the property was a good size.

"There are so many things you can do with the lot," Hannah said to his mom. "A courtyard. What do you think about the idea of building a garage with an efficiency apartment above it?"

"I love that suggestion, dear!"

Thoroughgood looked at Mason and nodded his enthusiastic support of the idea. For someone who said she didn't know a lot about houses, Hannah was a natural.

Seeming entertained, Thoroughgood pulled out his cell phone and began filming shots of the interior.

"You know, maybe you could pop the top. That's a thing, isn't?"

"Of this house, you mean?" Judith asked.

A natural, all right. And she knew how to double the budget in ten seconds.

"That's what I was thinking. That way you could double the square footage without needing to pour another foundation, or whatever you'd need to do," his little sub added, her entire body humming with vibrant energy.

How had she and his mother become in cahoots so quickly? Deborah's relationship with his mother had been lukewarm on good days, frosty on others.

"Like a master retreat kind of thing with a bathroom? What do you think, Mason? Is that possible?"

"Potentially." Mason took his time with an answer, being guarded. Hannah didn't seem constrained by reality. Instead, she was steeped in possibility, seeing what could be, while a million practical details swam through his head. "I'd need to get up in the attic to see. Consult a structural engineer."

He'd thought maybe Hannah would hang back while his mother explored the place, but she didn't. They walked together, discussing potential layouts and furnishings.

He wondered why he'd come along at all.

By some unspoken accord, he ended up in the space that was originally a kitchen with Norman and Thoroughgood while the two women walked outside, discussing the possibility of building a pergola.

"If you add curtains to it, you can block out heat or wind," Hannah suggested. "And an overhead fan would be perfect. Then you can use it almost all year round."

"I'm interested in this," Thoroughgood mused, following the women.

Reluctantly, Mason and Norman left the coolness for the outdoors.

"A magnolia tree for shade," his mom decided.

"How about a firepit?" Hannah suggested, pointing to the right.

Mason saw dollar signs, and he wondered if his mother had any idea how much her dreams might cost.

Ten minutes later, they all went back inside.

"What do you think, darling?" Norman asked.

His mother was beaming. "Actually, no need. I've made a decision."

"Have you?"

Hannah returned to Mason's side, and her body was warm from the late-spring sun. "I love this place. So much potential."

"John, offer him thirty thousand less than he wants."

Thoroughgood nodded very, very slowly. "I think that might fly, Ms. Sullivan."

"Mom, why don't you wait? Give me a day or two to run some numbers for you."

"Thank you, darling. That won't be necessary."

What the hell? All these years of her not wanting to expand out of her comfort zone, and now she wanted to buy a vacation rental? "You should look at a budget."

"Of course. We won't do anything extravagant. The market won't allow it. But John ran the comps. Even if I put a hundred thousand into renovations, we'll still be in good shape. And fortunately I know a builder who will be more than fair with pricing."

"At least get an inspector to look at it?"

She smiled. Norman shrugged helplessly, in an age-old male gesture. For the first time, he felt for the man.

"Let's go to lunch to celebrate!"

"I'm starving," Hannah agreed. "And I love celebrations!"

It took a few minutes to get everyone out of the house and lock the door.

When he and Hannah were inside the car with the blessed air conditioner running, Hannah grinned. "That was a lot of fun."

"You mean it?" Since he wasn't familiar with the restaurant Thoroughgood had suggested, Mason waited for the man to turn around his toy car and then followed him down the road.

"Most definitely. Now I can't wait to go to that walk-through with you."

"I was afraid I was ruining our afternoon."

"Not at all. That cottage is like clay, waiting to be sculpted. And your mom?" She adjusted one of the vents. "She's so sweet."

Deborah hadn't thought so.

"I love how close the two of you seem to be." Hannah turned to look at him, and she was wearing a soft smile. "It tells me what a good man you are."

She placed her hand on his thigh.

A need to possess her seared him. Hannah didn't know it yet, but he had no intention—ever—of letting her go.

CHAPTER 9

At the small restaurant that catered to locals with enormous muffuletta and po'boy sandwiches served with French fries and deep fried okra, Hannah sat next to Judith, while the three men huddled up to talk football.

"I do like your suggestion for the focal point," Judith said.

"A tiered fountain? Or a sculpture?" Hannah grabbed her phone, and they searched images of various Southern landscaping. Taking note of what Judith liked, Hannah began to doodle on a napkin.

Grinning, Judith took the pen and added some of her own touches.

"I think it's going to look wonderful. All those colors and things that flower at various times. And honestly, I might go for the fountain because the sound might drown out some traffic noise."

"Good point."

"And you could try to attract butterflies."

At that suggestion, Judith added a birdbath beneath a tree. "A glass one. Not concrete."

"I saw some at a garden center in Austin. They had

different designs. I loved the cardinal and blue jay." She opened the website to show Judith. "This one is my favorite." Hannah opened a picture of one that was a large, colorful dragonfly.

"Perfect. I'll order one."

"I can't wait to see how it comes out," Hannah said when their food arrived.

"You're going to be part of it. Don't think you're not getting your hands dirty!" Judith proclaimed.

Being welcomed into the heart of Mason's life elated Hannah. It had been a long time since she'd enjoyed using her creativity this much.

To complete the celebration, Thoroughgood ordered a serving of bourbon sauce–drenched bread pudding.

"Have some," Judith encouraged.

Hannah wrinkled her nose.

"Go on," Thoroughgood added. "Try it."

Since everyone was staring at her, she picked up a spoon and carved off a small section.

"Dip it in the sauce," Mason said.

Skeptically, she tasted it. The sweetness exploded on her taste buds. "Are you telling me I've been missing out on this my whole life?"

"I assume you like it," Mason teased.

"It's official. I have to live someplace where I can get this whenever I want it."

Leaning in so he wouldn't be overheard, he said, "You are more than welcome to stay."

An air of seriousness sliced through his words, making her shiver. Around them, conversation continued, as if her world hadn't lurched to a stop.

"Sorry to cut this short," Thoroughgood said a few minutes later. "I have another appointment."

"Us too," Mason added. "Meeting homeowners in Algiers."

They all said goodbye, with his mother promising to update Mason on the plans to purchase the cottage.

Outside, the heat was wilting, and Hannah was glad for the car's air-conditioning.

When she came to New Orleans, she tended to only visit touristy places, so she enjoyed seeing the various neighborhoods as they drove to the house he was renovating.

The neighborhood was gated, and the properties were so large they were more like estates. There appeared to be a mix of modern structures as well as historic-looking ones.

"This one was built in 1882 and reconstructed here in the early 1980s," Mason said as he pulled into the circle drive. "But it hadn't been touched since. This is the first renovation since then, and the Stevensons have an eye toward preservation."

Melissa Stevenson met them at the door and invited them inside. The home was over eight thousand square feet, and renovation seemed to be happening everywhere, making it difficult to see what the finished project might look like. She admired Mason's vision even more.

Despite the disarray, Melissa offered sweet tea and lemonade, and Brent jogged down the stairs to join them.

They all walked through the house together while the Stevensons shared their thoughts and concerns, and she'd admired the straightforward way Mason pulled out a notebook and jotted down all the changes they wanted to make to the design.

Back downstairs, in the kitchen, Mason opened his tablet and the file that held all the information about the project. He scrolled to the working budget and showed them the financial impact of their changes.

"Forty thousand dollars?" Brent asked. "On top of what we've already agreed to?"

"That's a minimum." Mason looked between the two of them. "Could be a little higher, but we can also try to shave a little off the price when we meet at the design center."

"I'm not made of money," Brent protested.

"It's our forever home." Melissa looked across at Brent.

"Forever is how long we'll be paying for it."

"What do you think?" Melissa asked Hannah.

"Me?" It occurred to her that the Stevensons had no idea she wasn't involved in Mason's business.

"Am I being ridiculous?"

"It's a lot of money," Hannah agreed.

"I think having a powder room for guests is a necessity, not a luxury."

As it was, there was a bathroom on the main level, but it was all the way at the back of the house and could only be accessed through one of the bedrooms. "If you change your mind later, it will be more difficult—and expensive to add it."

Mason nodded. "Less disruptive to do it now as well, since you're not living here yet."

Melissa and Brent looked at each other.

"We could delay construction of the pool house," Mason suggested. "That would give you plenty of room in the budget. In fact, it would save you some money."

"Same argument." Melissa shook her head. "Building prices go up. And it will be disruptive."

"And my mancave is going to be on top of it." Brent scowled. "I'm keeping the mancave."

Hannah took a drink of lemonade to cover her grin. A bathroom, that they might use every day, was less important than his private space.

"It stays," Brent reaffirmed, as if there had been any doubt.

"Do you need time to think about it?" Mason asked. "You'll also be delaying your move-in date by a couple of weeks."

Brent heaved a sigh. "I'm not compromising on my list."

Melissa looked at her husband. "And I want my powder room."

Mason betrayed no emotion. "You've reached a decision?"

"Mel gets what Mel wants," Brent said.

"In that case, I'll get the changes drawn up." Mason shook hands with both of the Stevensons.

"Do you ever get frustrated with your clients?" she asked Mason once they were back in the car.

"No. Every decision impacts their lives, and I try to remember that. The paint color and the countertops will be the first thing they see each morning. Even the lighting choices matter. Every time you walk into a room, you flip on a switch, right? Is it bright enough? Too bright? How many options do you want? It may seem minor, but it's how our homeowners will interact with their space three hundred and sixty-five days a year."

"It's just a huge contrast, I suppose, from the scope of what they're planning versus what your mom is thinking about." The Stevensons' pool house budget was more money than Judith was planning for the cost of her entire renovation.

He stopped for a moment while the security guard opened the gate and gave a faux salute.

"Working with a million dollars is not much different than tens of thousands. No matter the price point, there are compromises that have to be reached. And most homeowners make changes until the last possible moment. One of my managers says she's more a marital counselor than project consultant."

"This is so much more interesting than booking travel arrangements."

"I'm always hiring."

Once again, he'd caught her off guard and left her breathless. He couldn't be serious. And yet, he was so very tempting.

"I owe you a nice dinner after taking up your whole day with my work."

"Honestly, Mason. I enjoyed myself."

True to his earlier word, they stopped at the small market near his house. That was a first for her. Liam had never wanted to go with her, but Mason had shown endless patience as she'd looked at the regional selections and added half a dozen pralines to their basket.

"Now to get you back to the house. I have a few ideas for the afternoon."

At his purposeful tone, a shiver that had nothing to do with the cold air blasting from the car's vents went through her. All of a sudden he'd spiraled her back into a submissive mindset, and she couldn't wait to be alone with him.

~

"Oh, la, la," Hannah said with a grin after they were seated at a fancy restaurant in the Garden District.

They'd been given a wine list that was at least ten pages long and a menu that contained no prices.

Though it was still early, and the dining room wasn't crowded, candles flickered on the tables, and a jazz quartet played in one corner. "Fancy, Mr. Sullivan."

"Only the best for my beautiful submissive. You went above and beyond today."

He'd asked her to wear the black dress she'd had on when they left the club. He'd refastened her pearls and swept his approving gaze over her, lingering on her breasts, making her wonder what he was thinking.

"You impressed me. Pleased me."

Warmth spread through her.

"You weren't overwhelmed?"

"Not at all." She shook her head. "Your mom is a firecracker. So much energy. And Norman…"

"I'm interested in your opinion." He took a drink of water.

"He's in love with her, isn't he? In a gentle way. It's very sweet."

"They met at a grief class."

She tipped her head to one side, hearing an odd note of pain in his voice, mixed with something that might have been judgement. "Do you not like him?"

"It's not about that."

"No? Has he done something to make you concerned?" When he didn't immediately reply, she made a guess of her own. "Does it seem too soon after losing your dad?"

"It hasn't been all that long."

"Disrespectful to his memory, maybe?"

"It's more than that. I want to be sure she doesn't jump into something too fast." He rearranged the salt and pepper shakers. "Or get taken advantage of."

She smiled. "From what I saw today, she's a woman very capable of making her own decisions."

"I'll give you that."

"Is it possible that your parents talked about this before he passed? Maybe he didn't want her to be lonely. Perhaps he wished her all the happiness in the world."

Mason dropped his hand from the table to his lap.

"Your dad sounds like a thoughtful man. I'm sure it would have occurred to him. Maybe he asked her to keep living and enjoy her life."

"Potentially. You're right that my dad would have been considerate enough to think about her emotional future as well as her financial one."

"And Norman? If they met at a grief class, it means they were working through the emotions, right? Both of them are facing reality instead of pretending it didn't happen or that they're okay. They reached out for support." She paused, trying to be sure she wasn't pushing too hard. "Your mom and Norman seem happy together. You talk to her enough to pick up warning signs if there was anything to worry about. Maybe you can trust yourself. And her."

Hannah toyed with her salad fork, turning it upside down on the tablecloth. "That's something I want for my mom. Ever since she and my dad split, she's been alone. Over twenty years. She sacrificed herself for me. But now I'm not sure she knows who she is. I'd love for her to find a man like Norman. A companion. Someone to share the journey with."

The waiter brought the bottle of mineral water that Mason had ordered for them to share. After squeezing the wedge of lime into her glass, she took a sip. "I know this is hard, but think about it from your mom's perspective. She spent her entire adult life with your dad. It has to be lonely."

"Yeah." He drummed his fingers on the table. "Maybe."

"Cynic." When he didn't respond, she took a step into dangerous territory. "What made you that way?"

He was silent for so long she wasn't sure whether he would answer or change the conversation, maybe even hope for a distraction from their server.

"Her name was Deborah. She was my sub. Collared. Owned."

Hannah sucked in a breath. She should have expected something like that.

"Things were fine when she had a job, but after a year or two, we agreed she'd stay home."

"That's a serious relationship."

"It happened so slowly, over time, but she became emotionally demanding. Stopped seeing her friends. Blamed me for her unhappiness." He lifted a shoulder. "I'm sure I was part of it. I was working with Dad. Then he got ill. And, well...she gave me an ultimatum. We could have made it through anything. I was committed to her. To us. It's my way." His words were flat, as if they needed no further explanation. "I asked her for patience. I couldn't give up the time, hours, minutes with my dad. He didn't have long to live, and my parents needed my support. But Deborah resented my work schedule. I tried to be compassionate. I knew it had to be difficult for her to be home all day, alone, waiting for me to arrive. Not just a partner, but a Dom."

A master.

The conflicts on his time and his heart must have torn him apart. No matter how she looked at it, it was an unwinnable situation. "I'm sorry. That's not how it's supposed to work, is it? In a relationship, you're supposed to be there for each other. Keep each other safe from the world. Be a safe harbor. Supportive."

"Nice idea, isn't it?" He lapsed into silence. "I worked at home as much as I could. And I invited her to visit me at jobsites or the office. But she refused to drive or call a car service. I'd offer to pick her up so she could spend the evening over here while I restored the house with Dad." He trailed off. "Needless to say, she had no interest in spending time at my parents' house or, later, the hospital. One afternoon, Dad had chemotherapy. After dropping him off afterward, I decided to come home instead of going back to the office. I bought Deborah flowers to surprise her. I was the one who got a surprise. She was gone. Her collar was on the bed next to a pair of bolt cutters and a note."

Then with honesty that stunned her, he continued. "It said, *thanks for nothing*."

The harshness took away Hannah's breath. "God, Mason."

"I would have given her the world." His smile was nothing more than a ghost that matched the pain in his eyes. "She showed up at my mom's house right after the funeral. Among the casseroles and stories and sharing of memories, she took me away from a conversation with Thoroughgood to tell me she forgave me for abandoning her."

"Last night." No wonder… "You stopped to be sure I wouldn't feel abandoned when you left me alone in your study."

"When I'm with anyone, I'm concerned for their well-being. Especially yours, Hannah. I would never harm you."

Not intentionally, perhaps. And to be fair, it wasn't his fault she was in danger of losing her heart, the one thing she swore never to do again.

The server returned to the table with a large basket filled with an assortment of rolls and breads. "May I bring you a cocktail? Perhaps a bottle of wine? I can suggest one, if you'd like."

"Would you like a glass?" Mason offered.

She frowned, confused by his question. This morning, before they'd left the house, he'd brought her to the edge but denied her an orgasm. Several times during the day, he'd teased her, ordered her to play with herself in the car. She'd assumed they would scene this evening, but if she drank, they wouldn't be able to.

Again, as if sensing her dilemma, he said, "As long as you eat and limit yourself to one glass, we should be fine. I'm skipping it, but I'll leave the choice up to you."

"In that case, I'll pass as well. Thank you."

"Very well," the server said, accepting the wine list that Mason handed to him.

"I think we're ready to order?" He looked to her for confirmation.

Hannah nodded her agreement.

"Ma'am?"

She opted for a cup of the shrimp and sausage gumbo, along with a blackened catfish. Mason went with étouffée and their largest steak, drizzled in a rich sauce and covered with buttered crab.

As they waited for appetizers Mason talked about the construction trade and its numerous challenges, from the weather, to keeping his crews working all year, to dealing with building departments, preservation entities, and homeowners who changed their minds about what they wanted.

"And I have the opportunity to pitch a show to a Canadian company that specializes in home improvement programs."

She'd been reaching for a bread roll, but she dropped her hand.

"New Orleans is a favorite with their viewers."

"That totally makes sense. So much history, different kinds of buildings." Generally, when she visited, she and Fiona spent a lot of their time hanging out in the French Quarter, but today with Mason, she'd seen a lot of different kinds of architecture. "It's vibrant, isn't it? Culturally. And there are so many places that could feature in episodes, right?"

"If I don't do it, no doubt another firm will."

"What's your hesitation?"

"Time. I ran the business with Dad. And it took both of us. I have managers." He shrugged. "But it's not the same commitment. And shows with couples, partners tend to do better. Someone to play off. And a unique dynamic."

"I think you'd be great at it. If you wanted to do it."

Their appetizers arrived, and she sipped the flavorful

soup. "This..." She looked across at him to see him staring at her. "What?"

He grinned. "Enjoying your enjoyment."

"If you think this is something, wait until the bread pudding arrives."

"How do you even know they have it?"

"With warm bourbon sauce. Just something you should know about me, I always look at the dessert selection first and plan dinner accordingly."

"Hence the catfish."

She tipped her spoon toward him. "All those good looks, *and* intuition."

"Tell me more about what you do."

"Nothing glamorous. I work in the corporate travel office at Lux Computers."

"They're big in Austin."

"One of the largest employers, yes. And since it's a multinational company, we have salespeople, techs, management, and executives traveling all the time."

"You like it?"

"It's gotten to be routine." She broke a piece off a roll and dipped it in her gumbo. "But I'm at the top end of the pay scale. There are generally cost of living increases and sometimes a bonus, but if I want to advance, I'll probably need to look at transferring to a different department or leaving Lux altogether." Which wasn't something she wanted to do. "I like my coworkers, and the hours are good. No weekends or holidays, which is a plus." Paid time off was in line with the market, and the benefits were wonderful.

"You like living in Austin?"

"Yes. Such a great town. Amazing music scene. Great art. Food. Different than New Orleans for sure, but the barbecue is killer." But she hated the idea of going back to a city where she was reluctant to rejoin the kink community.

Now that she'd been with Mason and rediscovered the thrill of being with a Dom, she wanted more…at least an occasional scene.

For the next hour, they enjoyed their food and easy conversation before the valet brought around the car.

"Masturbate while I drive," Mason whispered in her ear before he closed her inside the passenger seat.

Once he pulled away from the curb, she pushed aside her inherent embarrassment and hiked up her hem. It was dark, and there was little traffic around. A person would need to be in a truck to see what she was doing.

Still, playing with herself in the car was far more difficult than she'd imagined. The safety belt was a challenge, and so was the angle. But none of that seemed to concern her Dom.

He gave her occasional heated glances that kept her turned on.

"Save your orgasms for me, Hannah."

Her pussy throbbed by the time they arrived back at his house and he gave permission for her to stop fingering herself.

When he helped her from the car, he lifted her hand for a gentlemanly kiss. "That scent needs to be all over my face."

As if she'd been scalded, her skin heated.

He held her hand as they walked up the path.

"I've been waiting all damn day for this moment" His words were growly as he closed the door behind them, then turned the lock.

Though Hannah shivered at his dominant tone, her toes curled and her pussy throbbed. "So have I, Sir." Everything about him—from his wicked commands to his courteous manners—appealed to her.

He captured her chin, then claimed her mouth with an untamed wildness that foreshadowed the evening ahead. Passion. Possession.

Since she was auctioned off, she'd been sucked into Mason Sullivan's vortex, and she wasn't sure she wanted to get away.

He swept her dress up and off, then lifted her onto the countertop. "Lie back, Hannah."

"But…"

He cupped her shoulder and pushed with inexorable force. He was a man who would not be denied.

This was so wrong, and so damn hot. Beneath her bare buttocks, the quartz was cold. The gleam in his eyes, however, was hot.

"Open your legs."

Her feet dangled over the edge, and he took her thighs in his hands and pried them apart. Then he licked her, sucked on her clit, plunged his tongue inside her, along with a finger. He overwhelmed her. Satisfied her. "Sir, this is impossible."

"Come for me, Hannah. Give it to me."

Shamelessly she pushed her pussy against his face in silent entreaty. He understood and gave her what she needed, a sharp slap. In a wave, sensation crashed into her. Then he rubbed it out and licked away the hurt.

In seconds, the pain rushed away, replaced by clawing hunger.

Desperate, frantic, she played with her nipples, tugging on them; then she lifted her rear off the counter. "Mason!" She screamed as she climaxed.

Hannah allowed her body to drop back against the quartz, and this time the coolness soothed her.

"That'll take the edge off," he said, brushing one of his fingers across her lips, painting them with her own juices.

Hannah had never been with a Dom—or even a man—this considerate. She was aware that he was ruining every future experience for her.

"I could eat your pussy all day."

Hannah wasn't sure she could survive him.

"Upstairs," he ordered, working an arm beneath her to help her sit up.

Before helping her down, he gave her a moment to let her head clear. He held her for a moment, then kissed her gently, the taste of her satisfaction blending on their tongues.

"You good?"

"Thanks. I think I can stand on my own now." *Maybe.*

He dropped his hands. "I want you to walk up the stairs in front of me. And give me a show."

"How do you mean?"

"Be a supermodel. I want to watch you move those beautiful hips."

His request made her a little self-conscious, but surely it couldn't be worse than going on the auction block.

"If you stall, I'll put a butt plug up there to be damn sure you can't walk straight."

When she'd climbed the first few steps, he whistled.

"Now shake it, Miss Hannah."

She thought she was over her self-consciousness, but she was very much aware of his lewd focus on her. Still, swallowing her hesitation, she exaggerated her movements.

"You're slaying me, woman. Dead."

She laughed. And because he was pleased, she relaxed and gave him more of what he was asking for.

"That's it. My sub."

At the top of the stairs, she turned toward his bedroom.

"Third floor," he said.

Curious, she stopped. "What's up there?"

"You didn't explore it yesterday?"

"No. I figured it was storage."

"Oh. It is." His words were as mysterious as his tone. "Go ahead."

Because these stairs were more twisty, narrower and steeper, she held on to the banister.

She turned the antique-looking key in the ornate brass lock and opened the door.

"There's a light switch on the left."

She flipped it up and illuminated the room. She gasped, unable to move. Standing on the threshold, a bit nervous to enter, she tried to take it all in. "Holy wowzer and a half."

He came up behind her to place his hands on her shoulders. "Do you like it?"

"You have your own dungeon?"

"Suffice it to say it wasn't part of the original design. It's a custom addition."

The floor was wood, polished to an amazing gleam. The wall opposite the door was painted a deep red that gave her a little chill. He had a spanking bench, and a structure that looked somewhat like a sawhorse.

There were two antique armoires next to each other, and he'd even thought to add a couch and a bed. Off to one side was a small sink and a couple of cupboards and bottled water on the countertop.

"This is..." *A fantasy come true.* Once again, she wondered how she could possibly endure a future without BDSM in it.

"When you're ready, go on in."

After taking a steadying breath, she did so, and her shoes were all but silent. "Soundproof, Sir?"

"Scream all you want, Hannah."

"I'm not sure if that's sexy or scary."

"Both, perhaps?" He paused for a frightening second before speaking again. "I'm going to paddle you."

She turned to face him. Damn, he was handsome. A lock of hair had fallen forward. He still wore a black suit with a bloodred tie. He was formidable and delicious. "Yes, Sir."

"Open the armoire on the right."

When she did, she found half a dozen paddles hanging from hooks in the top.

"Choose one."

Bravery deserted her. She bypassed the heaviest ones in favor of a thin leather one.

"Excellent. That's the same one I would have selected," he said.

After removing his jacket and placing it over the couch, he extended his hand.

Once she turned it over, she slipped into a different place in her mind. Her thoughts slowed, and her senses were enhanced. This was why she'd agreed with Fiona's suggestion to sign up for the auction. Hannah had missed living in this alternate universe.

"Nipple clamps?"

"Are you telling me to fetch them, Sir? Or are you asking if I want to wear them?"

"Wondering if they'll enhance your experience."

"Yes."

He smiled. "Same armoire. Middle drawer."

It was lined with felt, and a dozen pairs were stretched across the bottom. Enthralled, she selected clover clamps.

"Beautiful. Go ahead and put them on." He tapped the paddle against his open palm while he watched.

Under his scrutiny, each of her motions seemed exaggerated.

Placing the first clamp sent a spike of awareness through her, while the second made her moan.

"Pretty. So very pretty." He smacked the paddle harder, making her suck in a breath. "Now, walk over to the horse and bend over it. I'd like you to grab hold of the legs on the far side."

The sound of his voice had the power to make her damp.

The metal chain between her clamps caught on the top rail, and she flinched.

"Maybe we should add a weight to them?"

This time, she knew it wasn't a question. She was as petrified as she was intrigued.

Hannah had to stand on her tiptoes in order to situate herself as he wanted. The chain swayed, pulling on her nipples. She tried to stay still, but even breathing made them move.

"They were an excellent choice, weren't they?"

"Yes." They were. Nothing else hurt so good.

He crouched in front of her and tugged on the chain.

She whimpered.

"I love your sounds of distress." He placed a thumb beneath her chin. "It's like music for my soul."

Oh Mason.

"Not too much weight, but enough," he said, and she wondered if he meant the words to be reassuring. They weren't. He fastened it to one of the links. "Should I let go of it gently? Or just open my hand?"

Before she could formulate an answer, he dropped it.

Hannah screamed, rising up even higher and then instantly regretting it because getting back into position would force her to pull up on the weight.

"A lifetime of this wouldn't be enough." He moved behind her and tapped her right calf. "Please spread your legs."

Gingerly she inched her feet apart, trying to minimize the weight's movement. Even then, it seemed as if it made a gigantic arc.

Whose insane idea is this?

Mason rubbed her thighs and buttocks with more force than he'd used before, undoubtedly to increase the pressure on her nipples.

She was coming undone when he delivered the first stroke with the paddle, forcing her forward.

The explosion of pain rocked her world. "Yes…" she begged.

He continued methodically until she got lost inside her mind, a place where thought no longer existed. There was only pleasure—rippling, swirling, creating a kaleidoscope of patterns and colors.

She reached for them, became them.

Then shattered.

CHAPTER 10

In the middle of the night, Hannah woke up, and Mason's arm was wrapped protectively around her. They were in his bed, and her memories were a little fuzzy.

After the blazing paddling, she'd come back to reality. Her nipples were throbbing, but he'd removed the clamps and that horrid, satisfying weight.

He'd helped her into the shower before they fell into bed together.

On the third story, she'd turned herself over to him in a way she never had with any other Dom. She trusted him without question. And he kept her safe.

Because of that, he'd reached a part of her that that she'd closed off after leaving Liam.

That gnawed at her.

She'd traveled to Louisiana for a fun, kinky weekend.

She hadn't wanted to complicate her life by caring for a demanding Dom who lived hundreds of miles away.

And damn it, why did his mom have to be so wonderful too?

In the distance, thunder rumbled. Nothing terrible, just a growl blowing up from the Gulf of Mexico.

Maybe that had disturbed her sleep, but she doubted it. It was her feeling for Mason that left her wide-awake and unsettled.

Knowing she'd never rest if she stayed in bed, Hannah tossed back the sheet and eased herself from his grip. He mumbled her name and opened an eye. "I'll be right back," she whispered.

It wasn't the truth, but she was convincing enough to get him to turn over and go back to sleep.

From the closet, she picked up the T-shirt she'd discarded this morning and dressed herself in it as she crept down the stairs.

In the kitchen, she opened a bottle of white wine, hoping it would help dull the suddenly sharp edges of her emotions.

She carried a glass of the chardonnay to the living room and stared at the soft raindrops that were hitting the windowpanes and running down in fascinating rivulets.

A few sips of the wine didn't help her unwind. After setting the glass on a coaster featuring an image of a steamboat on the Mississippi River, she grabbed a throw and tossed it around her shoulders.

Still unsettled, craving the comfort of her own space to heal, she settled for turning on the television.

After surfing through all the cable channels, she switched to a subscription service and found a Christmas movie. It might be late spring, but with the storm and the frigid air from the air conditioner, she could pretend it was winter. And something to warm her soul would be nice.

More than halfway through the movie, a floorboard creaked.

A few seconds later, Mason stood in the doorway, sleep

tousled, fantastically handsome in a pair of loose-fitting black shorts.

To his credit, he didn't ask if she was okay.

Nor did he come sit next to her.

Instead, he eased himself into a nearby chair, at an angle to her. "I waited as long as I could."

She gave him a tremulous smile. It was the best she could manage.

"It's pretty powerful," he observed, voice hoarse.

"I'm sorry?"

"Whatever the hell it is that's going on between us."

A million words crowded her mind, some of denial, others flippant. And she didn't want to give any of them a voice. "I…"

"Unless I'm misreading the situation?"

She shook her head. "You're not."

Mason stood. He paced to the window, then back. "This is…" He stopped. "Damn. I made reservations for a jazz lunch tomorrow. And then I was going to ask you to consider staying."

The room seemed to spin. That wasn't possible. She had a life, had made promises to herself.

"You're scared."

Scared? Petrified. "I can't."

"Don't want to?"

"Won't." She wished the word had been forceful instead of a desperate whisper.

"You could consider it. Apply for jobs out here. I could help you find an apartment if you don't want to move in right away."

"It's not that easy."

"You can certainly work at Sullivan Construction."

He was so very tempting. But that was how she had ended up where she was. By not trusting her intuition.

Suddenly needing something to do with her hands, she leaned forward and picked up the wineglass. How could she make him understand? "I told you about Liam."

"The bastard." He nodded. "I'm not him."

"God." She blinked. "I know that. But I need you to understand."

He plowed a hand into his hair and left it there. "I'm listening."

"He would..." Thunder exploded and lightning slashed, making her jump and the lights flicker. Fitting. "We met at a munch. And it took him a couple of months to call me. We dated, and we occasionally went to a club in Austin. He seemed wonderful, thoughtful." In retrospect, he wasn't always courteous, sometimes short-tempered with servers and coworkers. Always, she'd made excuses for him. "We were together for over two years before I moved in with him." And she'd never considered getting a place together. Maybe it was intuition, but she'd always wanted to be able to escape. "After what my mom went through with my dad, I was determined not to get involved with someone controlling and manipulative. I needed to be sure."

Slowly Mason lowered his hand.

Rain fell in earnest, a rush, to churn things up and sweep the world clean. "I moved in with him. Not a dependent kind of thing. I kept my job and paid half of the bills. At first it was nice because we could scene more often without one of us going home afterward. Over time, things changed. It was so subtle I didn't see it right away. He started asking when I'd be home from the gym or from grocery shopping, and then he'd be angry if I was five minutes later. It became stifling. For him, though, it wasn't enough. He wanted to know where I was, who I was with. Then to assuage him, I had to keep my phone's GPS active so he could track my every move."

Mason dropped back into his chair.

"He found reasons to punish me. I'm a bit embarrassed about this, but I was able to rationalize it because we had a BDSM relationship. There are rules, right? And all couples are different. I told myself I was having difficulty adjusting to living with someone after being on my own for so long. Maybe I wasn't trying hard enough." She swirled the stem and watched the wine become a cyclone.

Still, Mason remained quiet, letting her go on—or not—at her pace.

It took her a while to decide to tell him the whole story, or as much as she'd told Fiona. The anguish, the fear, that was all hers to keep. "One night, his friend was over. Liam made me kneel—even though his friend wasn't in the lifestyle." Her voice cracked at the humiliation as she went on. "He chained my collar to a hook in the wall. And…uhm… they went out for the night."

He leaped to his feet. "Jesus Christ, Hannah."

"He let me go the next morning."

"The next…? What the fuck?"

"So it's not about you, Mason."

Another bolt of lightning shredded the atmosphere, illuminating the raw fury in his eyes.

"Fiona caught the first flight out. I picked her up at the airport. I left my phone at the office so Liam wouldn't suspect anything. We grabbed my essentials and that was all. She stayed with me at a hotel for a few days while I found a new place to live. I changed my phone number. And I've avoided scening so that I didn't run into him."

"I… Hannah…"

Raindrops ran like her sudden tears. "I need to go."

"Damn it. Look. Listen." He curled and uncurled his fist. "I won't make you stay. But I'd prefer it if you didn't go out in this weather. You can have the bed, and I'll sleep in the guest room. Or you can have any room you want."

"I'm sorry." It wasn't possible for her to be this distraught. She hardly knew him. *Tell that to my heart.* "I know you paid a lot of money."

He shook his head. "It's not about the money. Not even a little bit. You're priceless to me, Hannah."

If he hadn't been so wonderful, she might have really enjoyed their time together. But he wanted too much from her. And the worst thing was? She was tempted to give it to him.

"Stay the rest of the night?" he invited. "If you want, I'll just leave you alone with Bing Crosby. Then in the morning, I'll take you to Fiona's. Or, hell, you can call yourself a car. Whatever makes you feel safe."

The idea of running into the night was ridiculous. Fiona probably wasn't home, and if she was, she'd be worried when Hannah showed up.

Leaving in the morning made a lot more sense. Slowly, she nodded.

"Thank you." He exhaled a relieved sigh that told her how important her answer was to him. "Where would you like to sleep?" He extended a hand.

She took it, knowing she was making a choice she would regret later but needed right now.

Without her saying a word, he knew what she needed.

Upstairs, in his bed, he made sweet love to her. Then held her while she curled against him and cried.

~

"So when are you coming back to New Orleans?" Fiona asked. "Did you check your email from the Quarter? They just announced there's going to be a Western night theme next month that sounds like fun. Poker tables. Cowboys in chaps or"—she shuddered excitedly—"maybe tight-ass jeans.

Polished boots." She licked salt from the rim of her margarita glass. "There's going to be a bucking bronc."

Hannah grinned. That would be worth seeing. Undoubtedly, Tops would require their subs to climb aboard, wearing next to nothing. A club in Austin had one of the mechanical contraptions, and it was a ton of fun to watch, even when the participants were fully clothed. At the Quarter, the people who climbed aboard would be mostly naked when they were flailing about.

"Shelby said she might come, if David will take her."

As far as Hannah knew, the two were friends, and David had recently gone through a traumatic experience with a sub he'd fallen in love with. "What's with those two, anyway?"

"Long story. Want to hear it?"

"Yes." Anything to avoid talking or thinking about her own lonely life. "Absolutely I do."

This was Hannah's birthday weekend. When Fiona learned Hannah had no plans and was going to spend the weekend alone, she acted. With her usual take-charge manner, Fiona bought an airline ticket, and she'd purchased a luxury hotel and spa package in downtown Austin.

This morning, they'd had room service for breakfast. Then, over cappuccinos at a funky, hip coffee shop, Fiona had entertained her with details of her now three-week-old relationship with Mr. Snorebox. Fiona said he bought her a huge box of earplugs as a gift, and the two had settled into a routine, spending most of their time together, going to the club every weekend.

There was something different about Fiona. She smiled more, laughed faster…with a man she labeled as somewhat boring. It turned out that his steadiness was something she'd wanted all along. It grounded her, helped her focus.

They'd spent the rest of the day being pampered with a

catered lunch made from organic ingredients, then facials and massages.

Afterward, they'd dressed up and headed to Sixth Street for dinner and to listen to live music.

Now they were back at the hotel. Like many others, they'd gone to the lobby bar, but since it was too noisy to talk, they'd decided to have a second cocktail at the much-quieter upstairs bar overlooking the city.

"They're never going to be more than friends. Shelby doesn't like to go to the club by herself, which causes her a conundrum, right? Because she's with David, other Doms don't approach her." Fiona shrugged. "When he was with Janine—what a bitch—he didn't see Shelby. But since the bitch—I mean Janine—dumped him for Master Trevor, they're hanging out again. Anyway. You and Mason should come with me and Andrew."

Hannah stirred her margarita and stalled. This was the moment she'd been dreading.

"Don't think I haven't noticed that you change the subject every time I mention Mason's name. You did it when I was taking you to the airport, so I thought you needed some time to process. What happened between the two of you?"

True to his word, Mason had driven Hannah to Fiona's house first thing Sunday morning. Fortunately, she'd still been with Mr. Snorebox, so Hannah had spent the day alone. She checked on her flight, packed her bag, spent too much time thinking, wishing things were different. When Fiona bounced into the house, Hannah pretended she'd just arrived.

"Was he an awful Dom? Is that why Deborah dumped him?"

"No." Not at all. "He was…"

"I've seen him play. Amazing, right?"

"That's a good word." So much so that she couldn't stop

thinking about him, getting out her vibrator and replaying each of their moments together.

"So, how is this a problem? Why don't you want to see him again? Or wait! Did he not like you? That asshole! No taste at all!"

Hannah drew her untouched drink toward herself. "He's not an asshole."

Fiona pointed upward. "I knew it!"

"In fact..."

"In fact?"

This admission was hard. "I liked him."

The triumphant smile faded from Fiona's face, and she drew her eyebrows together in concern. When she spoke again, her voice was quieter, as if she was finally realizing her friend had been hiding something. "What happened, Han?"

"He asked me to stay."

"He asked you... Seriously? Wow. I mean, I get that he might come see you or that he'd invite you down again. I'm not surprised that he was into you. But asking you to stay? That's serious. And that's quite a departure for the One Night Dom."

"It scared me." And from the beginning, she'd been honest about what she was offering.

"Okay. So..."

Hannah smiled. Fiona always spoke like that when she was trying to figure out the right thing to say.

"Things must have gone well, right?"

Trying to decide how much to say, Hannah took her first sip of the margarita. The bartender had been more than generous with the tequila, and she coughed. "Wow. This will get all my secrets out of me."

"I tipped him well."

Hannah laughed. "I believe you."

"It's true." Fiona settled back and waited without pushing further.

"He's easy to be with. On Saturday morning, we went and looked at a house with his Mom and her boyfriend. He didn't think I'd want to spend time with his family, but it was so much fun walking through the house. It's in terrible disrepair. But so much potential." She wished she knew whether or not Judith had bought it.

She took another sip from her margarita. "He's working on a pitch for a renovation-type of program for cable."

"That would be cool," Fiona said. "Maybe I can get a walk-on part. Like someone who shows up for all the open houses or something."

Hannah, too, would love to be part of it.

"Were there any red flags that bothered you?"

"Other than the fact he wanted me to uproot my life?"

"Okay, I'll grant you, that's a lot. If it hadn't been for Liam, would you consider it?"

"It's impossible to discount that, though, isn't it?" She sighed. "I moved slow with Liam, and it didn't help. It turns out I never really knew him."

"Has it occurred to you that there were warning signs? Your intuition was screaming at you. Maybe that's why it took you so long to move in. You kept telling me you weren't ready. When I asked why not, your answers were vague."

Hannah considered that idea. Liam hadn't always been forthcoming about his whereabouts, and she'd caught occasional glimpses of anger that he'd shoved away quickly. No one was perfect. So she had pushed away her apprehensions.

"You're strong, Han."

She wrinkled her nose. "Not so much."

"Stronger than you think. You survived Liam. I think you can count on yourself to get through anything life throws at you."

The cost had been high. She'd kept to herself, insulated and alone, to protect her emotions.

Not that it had helped.

"I'm not telling you to do something rash." Fiona batted her eyelashes.

"But?" Hannah prompted.

"What's the risk? Really? You love New Orleans. You have no real attachments to Austin."

Especially not now that her mother had moved to Florida.

"It's worth considering. I'd really like having you closer. You can stay with me for as long as you need. Have a look at jobs online. And then…" She frowned. "No. Wait! I've got an idea. You are *so* going to appreciate my brilliance!" She brandished her straw, flicking drops of margarita across the table, not that she seemed to notice. "You can fly down for Western night and combine it with interviews."

How did Fiona make everything seem so easy?

"It's perfect. You'll have a chance to see how it goes with Mason." She toyed with her straw. "Maybe it was nothing and it won't go anywhere, anyway. But at least you'd know. Right? You could date without having to live with him. Take him for a test drive, like you would a car."

Hannah scoffed at her friend's ridiculous analogy.

"Don't you want to at least give it a try? Or do you want to spend your life wondering if something might have been possible?" She paused. "Or think about this. When you come for Western night, how will you feel if you see him with someone else?"

A chill seeped down Hannah's spine.

Fiona's cell phone rang, and she grinned, sliding around on her chair as if she were a schoolgirl. "It's Andrew."

"Answer it."

"Are you sure you don't mind?"

"Of course not." When Fiona still hesitated, Hannah picked up her phone and opened her favorite social media site. "Go!"

"Okay. But I'll be right back. Stay out of my margarita." Then she swiped her answer button, and her voice was giddy as she said, "Hi, sweetums."

Sweetums?

Fiona moved to the back wall, in the corner. Still, her friend's giggle was audible. Hannah shook her head. Until Mr. Snorebox, no man had made Fiona giggle.

Now that she didn't have to make a show of being interested in checking her notifications, she turned her cellular device facedown.

Fiona's words haunted her.

If she didn't reach out to Mason, she might never know what her future held. He scared the hell out of her, asked too much. And maybe she was too distrustful to even give him a chance.

But in the three weeks since she'd seen him, she'd never been more miserable.

A few minutes later, Fiona returned, all but skipping across the floor. And she was blushing. "You look happy," Hannah said

"I am. At least for now. And I refuse to jinx it. The novelty may wear off in a week, and that would be okay. Don't get me wrong, that's not preferable. I really like him, so I'm going to see where it goes."

Fiona had said Hannah was stronger than she realized, but she wasn't sure about that. Fiona was fearless in the face of potential hurt, something Hannah wasn't sure she was capable of.

"Here's the deal—if I get my heart broke, you have to help me pick up the pieces."

"I think I owe you one or two."

"That's what friends are for. Now that's enough of that. We're going to celebrate your birthday!" Fiona raised her glass. "I hope your year ahead is filled with joy."

"Thank you."

"Cheers, my friend."

They clinked their glasses together. The future was up to her, Hannah knew. *Am I brave enough to do something about it?*

CHAPTER 11

"Where's your young lady?" Mason's mother asked. "I thought she might come with you. I was looking forward to hearing what she had to say."

Along with Norman and Thoroughgood, they were back at the fixer-upper, and she had just secured the keys to the property. She wanted to have another look around and make sure she was still happy with the plans he'd drawn up for her. Like Hannah suggested, they were going to raise the roof and add a master suite and sitting area upstairs. Norman had suggested adding a deck, as well, to catch a breeze. Mason had to agree it was a good idea.

His mom's head was tipped to one side as she waited for his answer.

"She's back at home. In Austin."

"Texas?"

Despite the fact that the house had a good air conditioner and it was working just fine, he was suddenly a little warm. "You're not the only one who isn't happy about it."

"When is she coming back? She seemed lovely. Not like that other...one."

"Deborah."

"Bless her heart."

He grinned. He had long suspected his mother didn't care for Deborah, but she'd kept her opinions to herself.

"Be sure to let me know when Hannah returns. I'd like to see her."

The lie came easily. "I will." He didn't have the heart to admit the truth to either of her or himself. Hannah wasn't returning.

"I want to look at the backyard," she said. "Norman, will you walk with me?"

"Certainly, dear."

The man deserved a medal. Despite the ninety-three-degree temperature and stifling humidity that made it difficult to move or think straight, Norman hadn't hesitated.

"That's true love right there." Thoroughgood loosened his tie after the two exited through the back door.

"Glad she didn't ask us to go with them." He didn't need to be involved with the garden plans. He worked with some of the best landscape companies in the city, all of whom were better at design than he was. "How's the investment business?"

"Growing." Thoroughgood nodded. "Plans for your TV show debut?"

"Still a long way from that, my friend." He hadn't even thought about it since Hannah left. In fact, he hadn't done a whole hell of a lot of anything, except for hiring a crew to build the gazebo Hannah would never see.

"Is your house available for a fundraiser? I want to send a couple of kids to football camp."

"What are you thinking?"

"There was a lot of buzz about the house while you were renovating. I think we could sell tour tickets. Maybe champagne and caviar as a theme?"

"Happy to help." It was exactly the type of thing his father had thought about when making the purchase. Restoring it to its original splendor and opening the doors to share with the world. "I think you should find a few more homes. Five stops, if possible? Different foods at each? Champagne at one. Caviar at another. Chocolates. Cheese boards. Fruit. That kind of thing."

"This could be bigger than I thought." The man nodded.

"I can make some suggestions." He was sure his mother would act as his hostess, but it would be nice if Hannah were there to help.

"Okay if my assistant calls you?"

"Sure." How the hell would he juggle one more project?

"You avoided your mother's question."

Mason didn't reply.

"About Hannah. She made quite an impact."

Like his father before him, Mason had trusted Thoroughgood for many years. It wasn't just because of his financial advice, but also his ability to be objective about life events. Though he couched things in the gentlest of terms, he didn't hesitate to ask uncomfortable questions. He'd forced Mason and his father to face things they'd rather not—his will, end-of-life directives, funeral arrangements.

If anyone would understand Mason's dilemma with Hannah, it was Thoroughgood. And frankly, Mason needed a sounding board. The past few weeks had been some of the most difficult. Losing Deborah had stung, but she'd caused so much drama that part of him was relieved to go home at night and not face an argument.

But Hannah had been stable, a breath of energy he hadn't known he was missing. Often times, he imagined starting their day on the gallery, coffee in hand. Maybe followed by hot sex, just enough to hold him through the day when he could get back to her. "No idea."

"Something go wrong?"

"Moved too fast, maybe."

"False start?"

At the use of the football term—indicating an offensive player who moved across the line of scrimmage before the ball was snapped—Mason winced. "Should have allowed the game to progress at its own pace."

"There's a penalty for that, for sure. But the game continues." He clapped Mason on the back. "Unless you were an asshole, in which case, she should be done with you."

An asshole? He doubted even Hannah would call him that. Or maybe he was wrong. Impatient, for sure. He'd calculated badly, something he regretted every day.

He should have asked permission to call her, done the polite thing and courted her. Eventually he could have suggested she fly down for a weekend. Taken it slow.

But manners—his upbringing as a gentleman—had deserted him the face of her upset and what they'd shared.

During their time together, she'd offered her body and her submissive surrender.

The beginning of their relationship had been extraordinary, igniting his caveman responses. He wanted to stake his claim and protect her, slaying her dragons once and for all. When he tried, she pulled a protective shield around her heart. Instead of thinking it through, he'd reacted instead of taking a step back. He'd asked for a future while she was still working through her past.

His mother breezed back in, followed by Norman. "Hannah made several suggestions when she was here. About the courtyard. I can't find the napkin we did our drawings on. Mason, dear, do you remember what we decided?"

He shook his head. "Sorry. I have no idea." He'd been busy running a budget in his head, calculating if the house was going to be a disaster of an investment property.

"I'm trying to remember about the fountain specifically. She suggested it have a number of tiers. We discussed concrete, I think. Or maybe it was metal. And she had ideas what to plant around it. Suggested we try to attract butterflies."

"I saved a video of you two talking," Thoroughgood said. "If that's any help?"

"Oh John! You're always thinking."

He grinned. "I like to have something to refer back to. Memory's sketchy. Especially when you've taken as many hits to the head as I have." He pulled out the cell phone that was tiny in his massive hands. Since his fingers were too big for the icons, he used a stylus to find and play the video.

Everyone gathered around, and he held his phone in the middle of the semicircle.

The sweet sound of Hannah's voice rocked through Mason, making him remember her cries and whimpers.

Damn, he missed her all over again.

"Oh, that's right!" Judith exclaimed when they reached the part where she and Hannah were discussing the courtyard. "Thank you. Mason, do you think I could ask Hannah a few questions? Send me her email address or telephone number?"

"Sure, Mom." He was certain she wouldn't answer a message from him. But he could figure out a way to get hold of Fiona. If his guess was right, Hannah would be happy to speak with his mom.

The conversation moved on and didn't require his participation, which was a good thing because his brain was no longer engaged.

"I need to get going," his mother said. "Norman and I are going to painting class."

"Painting class?" He looked back and forth between the two. His mother beamed, and Norman grinned.

"Maybe we can use some of our masterpieces to decorate this place. Norman, what do you think?"

"Your…?" Mason ran out of words.

"Today's class is on sunsets. And they give us wine, too."

Thoroughgood cleared his throat. "Well, Ms. Sullivan, that's sure a nice idea."

Mason kissed his mother's cheek and shook Norman's hand, something that was becoming easier each time they met.

"We can't let her do that," Thoroughgood warned the moment the front door closed.

"Not if they want to rent it out, no. I'll let you be the one to tell her."

Thoroughgood shook his head furiously. "I think that's rightly a son's place."

"*You* are the family adviser."

They looked at each other.

"Those walls will look mighty nice with Judith's personal touches added," Thoroughgood mused.

"I'm sure they will." Mason adjusted the thermostat before they left the house.

Thoroughgood's words about Hannah haunted Mason as he drove to his office.

Maybe he'd given up too soon.

He wasn't sure how the hell to try again without scaring her more.

By the time he reached the office, he had an idea.

He called Thoroughgood. "Send me that video? I think Hannah will like it."

"You going to try for a touchdown with your lady friend, Mason?"

At this point, he'd settle for a three-point field goal. "Yeah. May take some time. But yes."

~

"I signed up for a dating site."

"Are you kidding me?" Hannah held the phone away from her ear for a moment, unable to believe her mother's words. "That's awesome. I'm so happy for you!" To her knowledge, this was the first time her mother had even considered a relationship since her divorce more than twenty years prior. Ever since, she'd focused on her job and providing for Hannah.

For a work promotion, Evelyn had recently transferred to Florida. Maybe the move had been a good one.

While her mother talked about some of the men's profiles, Hannah paced to the window and looked down at the pool area that was filled with people. Since it was a Saturday, a number of people were tanning in lounge chairs while others sipped cocktails beneath umbrellas. With the way the sun shimmered off the water, the whole area looked inviting.

Maybe when she ended the call, she should head down, spent some time outdoors. There were a couple of vacant tables in the shade where she could stream another episode of her favorite home improvement show. Ever since she returned to Austin, she hadn't been able to get enough of them. Last week, she binged the entire catalogue of one set in Texas, featuring a husband and wife who'd recently had their first baby.

She'd watched others that were hosted by a single person. Mason was right. The ones with a couple were more engaging. It was not just about the project. She'd become invested in the couple and their dreams for their future. In one episode, they sold their starter home and bought a derelict farmhouse on acreage. Each time the credits scrolled at the end, she clicked *start now* for the next one. She had to see how the little boy's bedroom turned out with its secret hidey-hole alcove. And she was dying to catch the big reveal of the master bathroom.

Realizing her mother had lapsed into silence, Hannah shook her head. "How's it going so far? Have you actually met any of them in person?"

"No. It's a complete waste of time and money."

"What do you mean?"

"All men are the same."

Her mom's words jolted her. Hannah had heard those words ever since she'd been a child. How much had they influenced and held her back? Was she guilty of believing that too?

Hannah exhaled.

Maybe. Maybe they had without her consciously being aware of it.

"They're selfish. Only after one thing, and you know what that is. As soon as they get it, they forget about you. Go find another skirt to chase. It's all there in their profiles. Everyone my age is divorced. What does that tell you?"

Before Hannah could respond, her mom continued. "None of them are interested in marriage. They are all looking for a good time. Like your father."

"Not everyone is like him." *Mason, for example.*

"You're smart to remain single, my girl. I closed my account before they could take any more money out of my bank."

"It couldn't hurt to chat with a couple of matches, if there's mutual interest."

Instead of responding, Evelyn changed the subject.

They chatted for a few more minutes, discussing mundane topics such as the weather and the wilting heat before Evelyn said she needed to go and throw in a load of laundry.

After they hung up, Hannah put the phone on the kitchen counter.

She genuinely wanted her mom to be happy, but suspected it wouldn't happen until Evelyn was willing to step out of her comfort zone.

Damn.

The realization rocked Hannah.

Ever since her return to Texas, she'd been restless. Every day, she went to work. A few times a week, she went through obligatory paces at the gym or went to yoga class. She'd joined her colleagues for happy hour last night, but nothing she did banished the loneliness.

Hannah told herself she was okay, pretended everything was fine when it was anything but.

The truth was, she was desperately lonely.

Maybe wallowing was okay for a while, but at some point, if she wanted to be happy, she couldn't allow her past to dictate her future.

She pulled her hair back.

Fiona was right. Hannah *was* strong. The first couple of months after leaving Liam had been rocky, but she'd managed. There was no doubt she'd have plenty of other challenges in front of her, but she could survive whatever came her direction.

She wanted to thrive. That meant seizing new opportunities, even though they came with risk.

Maybe she would look at job postings in the New Orleans area, even consider asking her employer if it was possible to work remotely. It might be possible for her to sublet her apartment in case things didn't work out.

She snatched up her phone again to call Fiona.

"Hey, girl! I was going to call you this morning, you know, when I wasn't tied up!" She giggled.

And Hannah knew her friend meant it quite literally. "I'm not envious at all."

"Liar. I bet your skin is green from jealousy. Like something out of a science fiction movie."

Maybe a little.

"Hold on a second, Han."

In the background, there were kissy sounds, and then Fiona squealed. "How about we talk another time?" Hannah suggested.

"No! I seriously was going to call. I just need to get out of this—*I'll be right back, Sir*—bed."

Hannah dumped out a cup of coffee that had sat too long. If she were in New Orleans, there was a good chance, she'd be sitting with Mason, outside, enjoying the breeze and a relaxed morning.

"Okay," Fiona said a minute later. "Any more thoughts about Western night?"

Her first instinct was to refuse. She shoved the thought away. That was safe, and the new Hannah was fearless. Or, well, filled with fear and willing to push through it. "I'll come."

"Holy shit! Really?"

As Fiona had suggested, it would give Hannah a chance to have some job interviews, if she decided she might want to leave Austin. "Really."

"That's awesome! You'll have my place to yourself since I'm not there very often anymore."

"Things have gotten serious with Mr. Snorebox?"

"It's so adorable. We don't want to be apart. We're thinking of wearing matching shirts to Western night."

Hannah grinned. Fiona's happiness was contagious.

"Anyway..." She took a breath. "Mason called me yesterday."

His name turned her heart rate sluggish. "Oh?" He was

thinking of her? After vanishing like she did, she was afraid he'd never want to speak with her again. She wouldn't blame him. "What did he want?"

"He asked for your phone number, but I didn't give it to him."

"Thank you."

"And, well, he sent me a video that he wants me to forward to you. I told him that it was your call and that I wouldn't do it without your permission."

Outside, people enjoyed their day while her world was tilting. "What kind of video?"

"I'm nosy enough to look at it." Hannah imagined Fiona was shrugging. "I'm looking out for you, after all."

"Right. Of course you are. What's it about?"

"I think you'll want to see it."

"Quit being a tease."

"Seriously, you're my best friend in the world. I think you should watch it without me saying anything. I'll say this. I think the One Night Dom has been vanquished. Call me back if you want."

They ended the call, and she held the phone in her hand, staring at the screen as if that would help the email arrive faster.

When her notification finally beeped, she sat on the couch to open the email.

Mason hadn't included any personal message, just an innocuous, *"I thought you might enjoy this. M"*

She touched the icon to play the video.

Mason, with his heart-tripping smile, filled the screen. "I'm hoping you enjoy this."

She reached out, as if to touch him, but that paused the video.

"Mom says thanks for the inspiration. And she'd like to run some ideas past you, if that's okay."

Yes. Mrs. Sullivan had been so warm and wonderful, and Hannah missed her. In fact, everyone had been lovely, John Thoroughgood, even Norman.

She touched the PLAY button again, then dropped her hand.

Mason's face vanished and was replaced with an image of the house she'd looked at with his mother. It continued with a tour of the inside. Hannah was in most of the shots, seen conferring with Judith. Vaguely, Hannah remembered John Thoroughgood documenting the day.

The final image was of Judith standing next to Norman on the newly built front porch, holding the key to the front door and grinning. Hannah smiled along with her.

Thinking that was the end, she sat back.

But it continued, with Mason's rich, dreamy voice in the background. "Demolition, well, what remains to be demo-ed, starts tomorrow. And construction will begin next week on the garage and apartment."

"Yes!"

"This is the design for the courtyard." He held up a drawing. "It was based on discussions with you, Hannah."

When he said her name, her heart pounded.

He zoomed the camera in.

Everything she'd discussed with Judith was on the paper. Courtyard pavers were arranged in a herringbone pattern. The landscaping was lush, with several birds of paradise, numerous gardenias, passion flowers, and her absolute favorite, angel trumpets. The enormous triple-tiered fountain stood on a circular slab that was surrounded by annuals. A glass table was set beneath a three-season pergola, covered with wisteria vine, complete with an overhead fan. And off to one side was a firepit, complete with inviting-looking Adirondack chairs.

She marveled at how gorgeous the artist's rendering was.

"I'm using this as part of the package I'm putting together for the home renovation show."

He was going forward with it? Delighted for him, she grinned.

"Of course, we can edit out images of you if you like, since I didn't have permission to use them."

No way. She was so proud to be part of the whole thing.

"If the show goes forward, I'm going to need a lot more help. So I'm posting a job opening soon."

There could only be one reason he'd sent her the video.

He was reaching out, inviting her to be part of his life in a nonthreatening way. She just needed to find the courage to leave her past behind and take a chance on the future.

The screen went blank.

He'd left the next step up to her.

CHAPTER 12

"You got this," Fiona said, braking to a stop in front of Mason's house.

His SUV was parked in its customary spot, meaning he was still at home. Hannah had no reason to hesitate, except for the butterflies that had leaped out of her stomach and were now tap-dancing up her spine.

"He's not going to bite."

Hannah fiddled with her purse strap.

"Unless you ask him to."

She laughed, and that relieved her nerves.

"I'll wait. If it doesn't go well, we'll head down to the French Quarter, drink hurricanes, eat ourselves into a carb coma, and talk shit about men."

"Okay. You're right. I can do this. Thank you." She wasn't sure how she had been lucky enough to find a friend as wonderful as Fiona.

Hannah had called her after watching the video, and Fiona wasn't surprised when Hannah announced she was flying to New Orleans to talk to Mason in person. Hannah had planned to rent a car, but Fiona insisted on picking her up.

Once again, Hannah was grateful for her friend's support.

After a fortifying breath, she exited the car and walked toward the house.

The gate was heavy, and, betraying her nerves, she fumbled with the latch before managing to open it.

Hannah had only ever entered the house from the back door, so she'd never fully appreciated the home's overwhelming grandeur until it dwarfed her.

When she was only halfway up the stairs leading to the porch, the front door opened.

She froze at the sight of Mason, grooves dug deep next to his jade eyes. His hair was a little too long and tousled. With his left hand, he gripped a sheaf of papers. He looked different than the last time she'd seen him. Exhausted, maybe.

"You're here."

Hannah attempted a smile, but it fell flat. On the plane, she'd rehearsed a million different openings. Some were casual, others a bit formal.

Now, looking up at him, they all fled, leaving her mouth dry. "I…wasn't sure…" She glanced toward the car, indicating Fiona.

"Weren't sure…?" In jeans and a golf shirt with his company logo, he was as handsome as ever. But the stark emotion etched in his eyes communicated his confusion. She understood, or at least thought she did. She hadn't responded to his email or let him know what her plans were.

"My luggage is in the trunk, and I thought I'd…" This wasn't going as she planned. In her mental rehearsals, she'd been confident, with a breezy air, instead of an emotional, stammering mess. "Well, I'm considering applying for a job in New Orleans."

"Are you?" A smile flirted with his sexy lips, softening his features. "Any place in particular?"

Humidity wilted her hair and her attempt to protect herself. "I understand you might be hiring."

"It's a partnership kind of position. More than an assistant, not quite an owner."

She was aware of Fiona staring at them, along with the mom across the street, the one who'd videoed her son's bike riding attempts. "I've been watching a lot of television shows about home renovation. I have some ideas for one that combines the best of them."

"You're only here for a job?" Where his voice had been welcoming, it was now a little tighter.

"No. I'm nervous."

"Yeah. So am I. I fucked up so bad with you last time that I'm scared shitless of doing it again, and I know I'm doing it again. Inviting you in might make you more nervous. Keeping you outside is unchivalrous. Fiona's car is running, so you're obviously not planning to stay." He wadded the papers. "Jesus, Hannah."

He dropped his papers on the table inside the door, then descended the single step that led to the porch. It was symbolic. She'd come to him, but he was meeting her partway.

But the rest was up to her.

"I told you—and I meant it—what happened that night was never about you. It was always me. You did nothing wrong."

"That can't be true. Otherwise you wouldn't have run."

"Don't you see? That was my choice. I could have asked you to slow down, told you I wasn't ready for that. Suggested we get to know each other better. Negotiated like we were in a scene or something. But when I saw how you reacted to what I told you about Liam, how fierce you were, I panicked, and I couldn't see past my fear." She tipped back her head so she could meet his gaze. "I've done a lot of thinking. I'm still edgy, and I can't tell you that all my past has been laid to rest. But I can promise to work on it. I mean…" She swallowed. "If you're still interested?"

"How could you doubt it?" His voice was hoarse. "I'm in love with you, Hannah. I'd do anything for you, climb any mountain. I've missed you. And I was so damn scared I'd never see you again."

Her shoulders rolled forward.

"You can set the pace. Stay with Fiona if you need to. Or get your own place until you're ready to move in. But I want to marry you."

She reached for the railing. She could see it. Wanted it. But everything about it terrified her.

"You haven't headed for the car."

"I'm not even tempted."

This time a smile slipped all the way across his face. "In that case…" He descended the couple of stairs to meet her, then swept her off her feet.

"But my suitcase!" She squealed.

"You won't need it for a while. I think Fiona will figure that out."

She looked back at Fiona. She'd rolled down the window and was blowing kisses. The couple across the street clapped.

This whole thing—homecoming—was perfect. And there was no place else she'd rather be. "Oh, Sir."

He carried her across the threshold and kicked the door shut behind him.

~

Mason looked down at the woman he loved. He'd been at the dining room table working when he'd heard the sound of a car. When the engine hadn't shut off, he'd been curious enough to investigate.

At first, he wondered if he was imagining the wisp of a woman walking up his path. But there'd been no doubt. Even if he were robbed of his senses, his soul would recognize her.

When he sent the video to Fiona, he hadn't been sure she would forward it. Even if she did, there was no guarantee Hannah would see it. If she did, how would she react? Delete it? Ask him to remove her from the video? Or recognize the truth, that together they were perfect.

He headed toward the staircase.

"Don't!" She threw an arm around his neck. "You…you're going to hurt yourself."

"No chance."

When they reached the top, he looked down into her eyes. "I'm going to give you a choice of what happens first. I can take you to the third floor. Or to my bed."

"I want you to make love to me."

So did he. Among other things.

In the bedroom, he slid her down his body, then closed the drapes and grabbed a condom before she undressed him.

Then, torn between feeding his hunger and wanting to savor every second, he sat on the mattress and watched her take off her skirt and tank top. Perfect sub that she was, she wore nothing underneath.

He crooked a finger, and she went to him.

Mason's cock was hard with incessant demand. She dropped to her knees and sucked him into her mouth, making him impossibly hard.

In the near future, he'd come down her throat, but for now, he wanted to orgasm deep inside her cunt.

"I've had a zillion fantasies," she confessed, looking up at him.

Since they'd entered the bedroom, the hesitation she'd

shown outside vanished. "I've thought about you every day." It wasn't possible, but he'd swear the scent of her lingered in his study, enough so that he'd even used the rolltop desk several times while she was gone.

From the beginning, the sex between them had been incredible. Their relationship might have bumps, especially in the short-term, but this was powerful enough to bind them together and help them get through.

He handed her the condom. "Please put it on me."

She did, and the way she handled his dick had him ready to rocket. Once it was in place, she stroked him, making him throb. Right now, it didn't matter that he beat off each evening in the shower. He had to bury himself inside her. "On your feet, woman."

Her smile was triumphant, as if she knew exactly the power she held over him.

He offered his hand up, and she straddled him.

"This is different."

He dampened a finger and teased her clit. Their eyes met. "You're already wet."

"I've been ready for you since you carried me up the stairs."

Still, he slid his fingers inside, and sought out her most sensitive space. She was so tiny that her feet didn't reach the floor while she was in this position, and when he pressed against her G-spot, she pitched forward, whimpering his name. "Now you're ready."

Hannah braced her hands on his shoulders, and he lifted her to settle her on his cock. "Oh God, Sir." She blew out a breath. "I forgot how big you are."

"The fit's nice, isn't it?"

She pushed back so she could look at him. "Yes, but I always seem to need a couple of seconds to..." She flexed her muscles to change their position a little.

"Does it help?"

"Not much," she admitted.

"Then I should give you something else to think about." He pinched her nipples, then quickly let go.

"Yes!" She lifted herself up a little, and he held her there for a few seconds.

Mason took a breath of her. In addition to feminine arousal and vanilla, there was something new about her scent. Hope?

"Sir, can we…?"

He lowered her on his shaft as he thrust up into her.

They found a rhythm together, and her breaths came in desperate gulps. Her hair fell around them in damp locks, while their bodies were slick with sex.

Hannah grabbed his upper arms, holding on, taking him as deep as he wanted to go.

To think how damn close he'd come to losing her.

The thought fucking destroyed him.

She allowed her head to fall back, eyes closed, lost in him, in them. "I'm coming, Sir."

"Do." As often as she wanted. A dozen times, and more.

Her climax was quiet, but she shuddered with her whole body.

Still grasping him, never intending to let go, he thrust up into her a final time, then came in long, hot spurts.

Keeping her close and safe, he moved them both so that they were snuggled on the bed.

"I've missed that. And you, Sir."

He pushed wayward strands of hair back from her face.

She was quiet, her eyebrows drawn together in a pensive arc. "I've never said this to anyone else."

Mason was content to wait for her to continue at her own pace.

"I love you."

"Can you say that again?" He grinned. "I'm not sure I heard you right." She could repeat herself all night, all day, and it wouldn't be enough.

"I love you, Mason."

"From the moment you first stepped onto the auction block at the Quarter, I had to have you. Then you looked for me."

She nodded, not denying it.

"And I knew you were mine." *To claim.*

"I'm glad." She placed two fingers on his cheekbone.

"I love you, Hannah. I'll love you forever. And I'll devote my life to proving it."

"Uhm... About the third-level dungeon, Sir."

"Master," he corrected, sending silence crashing around them.

"Oh, Sir. That's..." She met his gaze with her wide, beautiful eyes. "Are you sure?"

"Yes, my lovely sub." Finally Mason was ready for her to call him Master. He wanted the commitment it entailed, as well as the responsibility that went with it. "That is, if you find me honorable enough to deserve it."

"Oh, Sir." She swallowed deeply. "Master. My Master."

The words were so fucking sweet that his head swam.

"Please take me to the dungeon, Master Mason." She wriggled her way out of the bed, and he sat up to get rid of the condom. He caught her before she could get away, and he gave her ass cheek a slap meant to arouse.

Her breathing changed, slowing as she responded to him.

"Lead on, sub. We have lost time to make up for."

EPILOGUE

"Mason!" Hannah scolded as he caught her and picked her up. He carried her across their bedroom and sat on the edge of the bed. "We don't have time for this, Sir!" But she ruined her ferocious scowl with a giggle. She didn't want him to keep his hands off her, and in fact she guessed he'd respond exactly like this when she grabbed hold of his dick through his tuxedo pants.

"I always have time to ensure my beautiful sub behaves herself." Holding her tight so she couldn't get away, he upended her over his lap.

Hannah reached toward the floor in a desperate attempt to keep her balance.

He tugged up the hem of the gorgeous gown she'd bought for his mother's wedding, then rubbed her right ass cheek so gently she sighed.

When his touch became rougher, she tensed. Silently he was communicating what she should expect. She thought he'd be gentle, a tease and a promise of what would happen later tonight. But he fully intended to ensure the aftereffect of his actions lingered for a good long time.

"How big is my dick?"

What? She grinned. "Bigger than it was a minute ago, Master Mason."

"Smarty pants." He spanked her hard.

"Uhm… Nine inches, Sir?" Upside down like this, the blood rushed to her head, making it difficult to think. And he was being deliberately provocative. "Ten!" Then she became even more outrageous. "No, it's eleven, right?"

"We'll go with that. Since you awakened the beast, you can have one spank for each inch."

"Oh, it's seven inches, Sir. I know it! I was stroking your ego."

"You were certainly stroking something." There was love in his tone, but it was underlaid by his implacable Dominance, which pushed a shudder through her.

Mason was perfect for her.

She'd left her job in Austin and stayed with Fiona until Judith's apartment rental was built. Then Hannah had rented that. It was an efficiency—about the size of a nice hotel room—but it was enough. She spent most of her time either at Mason's house or at the Sullivan Construction offices anyway.

The home improvement network had green-lit several test episodes of their show. Producers had been intrigued by Mason's long ties to the New Orleans area, and the fact that he was courting Hannah added a dimension they thought might intrigue their audiences. When Mason announced he was going to do everything possible to get Hannah to agree to marry him, the production team had looked at each other, then nodded as they asked for rights to film the wedding and the release of exclusive photos.

Mason had agreed, so long as any proceeds went to his charity.

Planning, filming, buying properties, dealing with the

city, and all the inevitable construction delays was as exhausting as it was exhilarating. Mostly, though, she loved working with Mason.

He was a perfect gentleman.

Except for when he wasn't.

He raised a knee, tipping her forward enough that she flattened her palms on the floor. "We are supposed to be at your mom's place in twenty minutes!"

"You should have thought of that sooner."

Judith and Norman's autumn wedding was being held in the courtyard of the renovated cottage.

A camera crew from the home improvement network was going to be on hand. And the reception would be in the home itself—the first time anyone had seen the inside. Judith hoped that pictures and the buzz about the renovation would help the rentals get off to a good start.

Mason lit up Hannah's ass.

She gasped from the sudden shock. "Good God, Sir! What the hell was that?"

"Your new paddle." He held it in front of her face.

It was short, somewhat stout, and polished to a high gloss. And his name was carved into it.

"Do you remember, that first night at the Quarter? You liked one of their paddles?"

"Vaguely." It was difficult to think of anything past the shock to her rear end.

"I was going to buy it for you, but I decided right then that I wanted to make one for you. Something unique to us. Something memorable."

"This is why you've been spending so much time in your workshop?"

"A present for you, Hannah. Yes."

A present?

He paddled her again.

She screamed.

"I should have taken you upstairs. Keep it up, and I will."

He blazed her again, and she clamped her mouth closed.

For a moment, he stopped and traced the shape of an M on her skin. At least she thought that was what he was doing.

Mason delivered a swat that seared all the way through her body, rocketing tension deep into her muscles.

Unceasingly he continued. After each stroke, he outlined a letter of his name. "Your ass is so damn red."

Often he would give her some strokes on her upper thighs, but this time he was relentless in catching her in almost the same spot over and over again. The diabolical Dom probably intended that his full name be visible through the entire wedding.

When he stopped and rubbed her skin, she was sobbing. Her hair had come loose from its updo, and she was sure mascara was streaked down her face. Still, his touch reassured her and helped their connection to grow. Even though it shouldn't be possible, every day she loved him more.

After a few moments, she tried to push herself upright, but he placed a hand on her middle back to force her back down.

Hannah struggled for breath as he traced his entire name across her buttocks.

"We should start every day like this."

"I'd never be able to sit down, Sir!" she protested.

"Oh, Hannah. I can solve all your problems. It just takes some creativity. For example, you can kneel, stay like this, bend over the spanking bench, or in a pinch, I can secure you to the Saint Andrew's cross."

Another *gift* he'd given to her.

"At all other times, we can stay in bed."

"You really have thought it through, Sir."

He helped her up, then and kissed her deeply, with his

own promise for their future. True to his word, he had never pushed her to move in or even accept an engagement ring. Instead, he allowed her to set the pace, coming over when she wanted, staying if she chose. As a result, they were almost never apart. In this moment, content and protected, she knew she wanted to be with him forever.

~

"Congratulations, Mom."

Judith adjusted the boutonniere on the lapel of Mason's tuxedo jacket.

Guests had already arrived for her wedding and were seated outside in the courtyard of her recently purchased vacation rental home.

For two days, the crew that Hannah had hired spent their time decorating both the inside and outside of the house. The pergola was wrapped with tiny twinkling fairy lights and white ribbon, and each post was adorned with a large bow.

The triple-tiered fountain was a gorgeous focal point of the yard, and the area surrounding it was ablaze with colorful flowering plants. No detail had escaped her eye, and even the chairs were decorated.

"There. That's better," Judith said.

Even though it was her day and he was preparing to escort her down from the master bedroom that was being utilized as the bride's room, she was still his mother. He grinned. "I'm happy for you."

"I know the adjustment has been difficult, and I'm sorry for that."

"Maybe it was." He shrugged. But Hannah had helped him see the situation from a different viewpoint. Gentler. Move loving. "Norman's a good man."

Judith looked at her engagement ring. "After your father..." She paused to blink away sudden tears, and he saw her life in a whole new light...her loneliness and heartbreak.

His parents met when they were both in high school and had been sweethearts all through college before marrying straight afterward. Their love and support for one another had been unconditional. Impossibly, it seemed to grow deeper with each of their struggles. In all ways, they'd been devoted to each other.

"Well... I never thought I'd fall in love again." She gave a sunny smile. "It's not the same. No one could ever replace your dad or his place in my heart. But to have someone to share life's ups and downs?" She took his hands. "Someone who cares for you and shares the journey. I wish that for you also, Mason."

The experience with Deborah had hardened him. But Hannah's gentleness had replaced hurtful memories with new ones.

In the beginning, he saw how deep she'd buried her secrets, and he'd been determined to excavate them.

But her steadiness had changed him.

He spent time thinking of ways to make her life better, encouraging her, being there at the end of a long day, trying to make himself into a man who deserved her love.

"Oh, and he makes the coffee every morning."

He grinned. Trust his mom to put everything in perspective. "That's worth a lot, right?"

There was a knock on the door so loud that it could only come from Thoroughgood's large hand. "We're ready for you!"

"Come in," Judith called.

"Wow." He blinked. "You look radiant, Ms. Sullivan. Soon to be Mrs. Williams."

"Why, thank you, John."

"Anyway." He ran a finger behind his collar, then twisted his bow tie. He'd beamed when Norman asked him to stand as best man. But he'd objected often and loudly about needing to wear a penguin suit, complete with a pretty pink boutonniere. "Your groom is pacing out there. He's afraid you changed your mind. Might want to show a little mercy."

Judith smiled. "Can't have him fretting."

"I'm gonna head back down, reassure him. Hold him up if necessary."

"Ready?" Mason asked once Thoroughgood left the room. "New beginnings."

Downstairs, she picked up the bouquet of flowers that was waiting on an end table.

"I love you, Mom."

"So proud of you, Mason. And so was your dad. I love you."

He opened the back door, and when they were both outside, she tucked her arm into his.

"Please stand for the bride," the minister said.

When Norman saw Judith, he beamed.

Yeah. Everyone deserved happiness.

"Shall we?" Together, they walked down the path.

Hannah was seated in the first row, and she took Mason's breath away. It wasn't just the gorgeous gown or her smile. It was the love reflected in her eyes.

He couldn't wait to make her his.

Mason and his mother stopped in front of the minister, beneath the pergola.

"Who gives this woman to be lawfully wedded?"

Mason glanced at his mother, then Norman, before proudly announcing, "I do." He transferred her arm to Norman's, then stepped away to sit next to Hannah.

She reached for his hand and squeezed it reassuringly.

The ceremony was short, the vows they'd written were

beautiful, and the day was good practice for the wedding he hoped to have soon.

After the bride and groom were introduced to the guests and everyone clapped, he leaned toward Hannah. "You did a beautiful job. Willing to bet bookings for this house soar. And it will be a great wedding destination."

"It's about hiring the right experts." She grinned. "And I totally know the best in the business, Mr. Sullivan."

"I'm proud to have you by my side."

A catered meal was served. Then, as the sun set, fairy lights came on, twinkling along the edges of the pathways, the gardens, and the pergola. Floodlights illuminated the breathtaking fountain, and a live band struck up music. Later, when they began a ballad, he stood and offered his hand. There was only one way this evening could be any more perfect. "Will you honor me with a dance, my beautiful Hannah?"

"I would love to."

Though there were two other couples on the makeshift dance floor, it was easy to pretend they were alone beneath the stars and partial moon.

He pulled her into his arms, then brought her just a little closer still. "I'm in love with you, Hannah."

She looked up, a tendril of hair curled onto her cheekbone. "Oh, Mason. I love you so much."

"Marry me?"

Hannah missed a step, and he was there to steady her. "Marry you?"

"Surely it can't be a surprise." He struggled to suppress his grin at her wide-eyed expression.

"But…" She looked around.

"This is about us, not anything else." The proposal had been prompted by the romance of the evening, but he'd been planning it regardless. He intended to spend the rest of his life with her, treating her with the appreciation she deserved. He'd learned from his mother that life did mean risk, but love was worth it.

He moved her off to one side, where they had a little more privacy from the lights.

"You caught me off guard."

"But?" His heart rate turned sluggish. Did she need more time?

She tipped her head back. Her stunning eyes were more gold than ever, and tears swam in their depths. "This whole night is magical."

"Oh God, Hannah. Tell me that's a yes. Please?"

"Mason, from the moment you bought me, there's been no one else for me. You healed places I didn't know were broken. Yes. Yes, I'll marry you. Yes, I want to be your wife." Her voice cracked with emotion, and her beautiful tears splashed onto her cheeks. "Yes, I want to be your submissive."

He thumbed one of them away. "And my partner? The person I trust more than anyone in the world? The woman who will share her deepest secrets and greatest desires?"

"A thousand times yes."

Then in privacy of their own making, he claimed her mouth. "You've made me the happiest man in the world."

"I never imagined life could be this wonderful, Sir." She surrendered to a second kiss.

"We'll shop for a ring tomorrow?"

"And announce our engagement later, so we don't take anything away from your mom's day."

"Agreed." Mason had been right earlier. Having her agree to marry him had made the evening perfect.

She placed her head on his shoulder, and he wrapped his arms around her. And then he realized it wasn't just a perfect evening. She'd made his entire life perfect.

COME TO ME

If you like two sexy, dominant alpha males, a steamy touch of BDSM, some great suspense, and a heart-wrenching second chance at love, this is the story for you! It's a standalone novel with my personal guarantee of a magical happily ever after!

"The chemistry in this is off the charts hot!" Goodreads reviewer

SNEAK PEEK OF COME TO ME

Wolf Stone, no matter how drop-dead gorgeous he was, was out of his freaking mind. And an asshole to boot. "You left Nate out there?" Kayla Fagan demanded. "Have you seen the weather?"

"He's not made of sugar."

"If this is how you treat your fellow operatives, what do you do to your enemies?"

He shrugged. "None of them left alive to tell." He smiled, and it did nothing to soften his features. The quick curve was more wicked than anything, making his eyes darken, reminding her of those few moments of twilight before the sky devoured the sun.

He strode from the kitchen, and she followed. "Mr. Stone—"

"Wolf, or just Stone." He didn't slow down. "And I'm not worried about how I'll sleep tonight." He crouched in front of the hearth, tossing kindling into the empty fireplace grate.

Even though she was stunned by his bad behavior, she couldn't help her fascination as she watched him. His shoulders were impossibly broad. Long black hair, as wild as he was, was cinched back with a thin strip of leather. And Lord, he had the hottest ass she'd ever seen.

Thunder cracked, and she worried about Nate. "I think you should at least invite him in until the storm passes." Even though it was summer, weather could be extreme at this elevation.

"Save your breath." Stone struck a match, filling the room with the sharpness of sulfur. "My mind is made up."

"You can have a heart, just until the weather clears. Then you can go back to your regularly scheduled…" She stopped short of saying assholeishness. "Grumpiness."

His mouth was set, brooking no argument. "Let it be."

Huge splatters of rain hit the floor-to-ceiling windowpanes.

Wolf might be able to sleep at night if he left his comrade out there, but she would toss and turn with worry.

Decision made, Kayla crossed to the hallway closet, pulled open the gigantic golden oak doors, and took out a raincoat. She also grabbed her gun and checked it before tucking it into her waistband. She snatched up a pair of compact binoculars and a compass and was shoving her arms in the sleeves of the yellow slicker as she walked through the great room on the way to the back door.

"What do you think you're doing?"

"Exactly what you said. I'm saving my breath." Kayla spared him a glance. "I decided not to argue with you."

"Stop right there."

He spoke softly, but his voice snapped with whiplash force. Despite herself, she froze. She'd faced untold danger, but this man, unarmed, unnerved her. A funny little knot formed in the pit of her stomach.

Kindling crackled as fire gnawed its edges.

"Turn around." His voice was terrifying in its quietness. "Look at me, Fagan."

Struggling not to show the way she was trembling, she turned.

He stood. "I will be very clear, Ms. Fagan. You are here at my pleasure." He took a single step toward her. "I will not be disobeyed."

His statement was loaded with threat.

Wildly she thought of the room in the basement, the one with crops and paddles hanging from the walls. The one she'd been forbidden to enter, and the door she'd opened the first time he'd left the house.

She locked her knees so she didn't waver. "I've never been much for obedience."

"Nathaniel Davidson is far from helpless."

"He's a fellow member of the team." She pivoted and walked away.

The wind whipped at the door, nearly snatching it from her hand.

She turned up the collar of her ineffective raincoat. There was never anything friendly about a Rocky Mountain storm.

Fortunately, she didn't have far to trudge. In less than fifteen minutes, the ground beneath her sizzling with electrical ferociousness, she saw a streak of orange.

She grinned.

Members of her team were smart. Nate had donned a reflective safety vest. That would, at least, stop friendly fire.

"Davidson!" When she got no response, she called out a second time.

He started toward her. "Come to rescue me, have you?" he shouted above the roar of the wind. "Bet Stone told you to come."

"He sends his regards and invites you to sit next to the fire while he pours you a cognac."

Nate laughed. "How much trouble are you in for coming after me?"

"He didn't threaten to flay the skin from my hide."

"Doesn't mean he won't."

"Thanks. That's a comforting thought."

Thunder crashed.

"I ought to write both of you up."

Wolf. Her breath threatened to choke her. How much had he overheard? It shouldn't have surprised her that he'd followed, that he'd effortlessly covered the same ground she had in far less time. The man was in shape, and he kept himself sharp, the same way he had when he led American troops in the Middle East.

Over the lash of the summer storm, his voice laden with command, he said, "Both of you, back to the house."

The wind snatched a few strands of hair and whipped them against cheekbones that could have been sculptured from granite. His jaw was set in an uncompromising line. Out here, in the unforgiving elements, he appeared even more formidable than he had in the house.

Nate glanced at her. "Maybe I will get a cognac after all."

"No fucking chance," Stone fired back.

Cheerfully, as if he couldn't have been happier, Nate whistled and gamely started down the mountainside. No one should be happy about this kind of reception.

"Move it, Fagan," Stone instructed, leaning forward so he could issue his command directly into her ear.

"Yes, sir."

Steps short but sure, she followed Nate, leaving Stone to bring up the rear.

Minutes later, the mean-looking sky unleashed a torrent. Earth became mud. Rocks became as slick as ice.

She lost her balance, and Stone was there, wrapping an

arm around her waist, pulling her up and back, flush against the solidness of his body.

The sensation zinging through her was from him, not the streak of lightning. "I'm good. Fine."

He held her for a couple of seconds, his warm breath fanning across her ear. What would happen if she leaned back for just a bit longer and allowed herself to be protected in his strong arms? To feel his cock against her? To surrender to the fantasies that kept her awake at night and her pussy damp, even now?

And what fantasies they were.

Last night's sight of his semierect dick had driven her mad.

After he returned to his own room, she'd thought of the crops and paddles in his downstairs room. She'd pictured him using them on her while she gasped and strained, and ultimately surrendered to the inevitable. Turned on and needy, she'd pulled up her sleep shirt and parted her labia to find her clit already hardened.

She'd come with a quiet little mew and wanted nothing more than to scream the house down as his cock pounded her.

What was wrong with her? She couldn't afford thoughts like this with any man, particularly one she was sent to protect. Because of the risk inherent in working for Hawkeye Security, many employees were fueled by adrenaline, and affairs were common. But everyone knew the rules. No commitments. No emotions were allowed to get in the way of the job. But the way he held her was an invitation she wanted to accept.

When he released her, a chill crept under her jacket. This time, being more careful, she followed Nate's path.

The trip up had taken maybe about fifteen minutes. Down took half an hour. And by the time they reached the home's patio with its outdoor kitchen and oversize hot tub, the sky was spitting out pieces of ice in the form of hail.

Very polite country, this.

Minding her manners, she took off her shoes and left them on a rubber mat, then hung the slicker on a peg.

Kayla told herself two lies. First, that she wasn't stalling. Second, that her fingers were shaking because of the cold weather.

Stone unlocked the back door and indicated she should precede both men into the kitchen.

Nate followed her, and then Stone relocked the door behind them.

"You." Stone pointed a finger at Nate. "What the hell were you thinking?"

Nate took a step back for self-preservation.

Both men dripped water and tracked mud. Neither seemed to care. And neither seemed to notice she was even there.

"You knew I wouldn't invite you here."

Nate shrugged. "You don't want anyone. Because you're a fool."

"A *fool?*"

"For always thinking you can do it alone. And you damn well know it."

The men were a study in contrast. Fair to dark. Alpha to beta.

"Fuck your ego, Stone. There's no place I'd rather be." Nate's tone was flat, as if that explained everything.

Kayla sucked in a breath when Wolf devoured the distance to pin Nate against the counter. Nowhere to run. Nowhere to hide.

"Wolf," she said, licking her lower lip.

"You." He shot Kayla a frightening glance. "I will deal with you directly."

Her stomach plummeted to her toes. She was watching two magnificent warriors spar, and if she wasn't careful, she'd be collateral damage.

To find out more about Nate and Kayla, check out Come To Me HERE.

OTHER TITLES BY SIERRA CARTWRIGHT

Titans

Sexiest Billionaire

Billionaire's Matchmaker

Billionaire's Christmas

Hawkeye Series

Come To Me

Trust In Me

Meant For Me

Bonds

Crave

Claim

Command

The Donovans

Bind

Brand

Boss

Mastered

With This Collar

On His Terms

Over The Line

In His Cuffs

For The Sub

In The Den

Master Class

Initiation

Enticement

Individual titles

Double Trouble

Shockwave

Bound and Determined

Three-Way Tie

Signed, Sealed, and Delivered

His to Claim

Hard Hand

Printed in Great Britain
by Amazon

23754352R00119